THE BIG UGLY

THE BIG UGLY

John Woods

Woods publishing   Tucson, Arizona

This edition was prepared for publication by
Ghost River Images
5350 East Fourth Street
Tucson, Arizona 85711
www.ghostriverimages.com

ISBN 978-1-7338435-4-6

Library of Congress Control Number: 2019917394

Printed in the United States of America
December 2019

Contents

Dedication

For Bunker de France

Thanks Bunker. Couldn't have done it without you.

"I do. Why'd you stop for me?"

"I passed by you before you reached the Rest Area. You have a strong walk, you're a good-looking young guy but you're sweaty, smelly, and when we get to the motel you will shower while I run your dirty clothes through the washer/dryer."

• • •

Early dawn, they awoke and went at it again. Sated, Teena said, "You have a nice body. The first time you went off almost immediately, like a firecracker, the second time was lots better, and this now is a wow. You learn fast."

Chris thought, *I've died and gone to heaven.*

"After I buy you breakfast," Teena said, "I'll drive you to where you can find work as a fruit picker. I love having sex with you. But you're younger than I realized. I'm insatiable, you're jailbait, and that's a bad combination."

• • •

He felt free. He picked apples until the apples were done, then moved on to picking cherries. When the cherries were done, and pleased to note that he had added to his account, still thinking about the trick he would pull when he joined the Army, he began the walk back down Highway 82 to where it cut back into Highway 90 and he could then head East.

Chris stopped at each Rest Area since it allowed those also having stopped to get a good look at him and check him out. He turned down all offers of lifts from guys, but at the Rest Area east of Ellensburg, Christina Howell, heading back to Eastern Washington University, slowed down her brand-new Buick and offered him a lift.

He thought, *Wow! Life away from Mom, how sweet it is.*

• • •

He took a job for a time in Missoula repairing railroad track, what was known as being a gandi dancer, until cold weather started setting in. He picked up his last paycheck, and then headed south.

CHAPTER TWO—Chris's Story

Years later, Chris, the scar-faced soldier boy, still in uniform, having a hearing aid in his left ear, was sitting on a bench in New York's Union Square Park and watching the pigeons scrambling for the grain being tossed to the ground. He mused, *I never felt more alive, more in tune with my team, than when in combat. Now I'm alone.* These pigeons are less alone than me.

He asked the old guy feeding the pidgins and sitting across from him, "There a hotel near here?

The old guy nodded, said, "I'm Harvey."

"I'm Chris."

Harvey pointed, "That's University Avenue. Two blocks down you'll find the Albert Hotel. They've got everything there, retirees, gay, straight, students, male and female prostitutes, actors, disabled vets like you and me. Everything. How much disability they give you?"

"Twenty-five percent. Sounds like my kind of place."

• • •

Two young men on the subway platform were goofing around and making others nervous when the scar-faced soldier boy, Chris Cordel, came through the turnstile. He was in uniform, had a hearing aid in his left ear, combat ribbons, a Purple Heart, and a Silver

or perhaps chose not to notice, that he had bought a backpack, a bedroll, and a road map.

Tim, his mother's latest, had sad knowing eyes, and Ray suspected that Tim had already recognized that his marriage had been a mistake.

In public, Chris's Mom played the part of the loving mother, and spoke glowingly of how proud she was of her son. In private, sometimes she was playing the role of a kind and loving mother and sometimes she was not. When not, she would say, "Chris, do you realize what my life could have been if it weren't for you? If it weren't for you I could have married the richest man in western Washington."

When his mother was half-drunk and angry she might even tell the truth, so this day Chris asked, "Mom, what ever happened to my little dog Toby?"

"I took that mangy mutt to the pound."

Walking away, Chris said over his shoulder, "Motherhood is a beautiful thing!"

• • •

On graduating the ninth grade, Tim (his Mom's Latest) gave Chris a hundred dollars while saying, "Don't tell your mother."

Chris didn't need it but the gesture moved him… seemed to uplift, make life seem worthwhile, and he had a plan.

• • •

Chris gave up his paper route on Friday. Saturday morning, knowing that the apple picking season was about to start, Chris arose early, showered, and left a note saying, 'I'm taking off for San Francisco.'

Ritch packed up a second set of clothes, caught the downtown bus, and was let off four blocks from the Greyhound Bus Terminal. He bought a ticket for the 25 mile trip to North Bend. He was heading East, not South. Easing back on the seats he reviewed in his mind the film he had seen where a Marine company had just finished their 30 mile march and were being loaded up on trucks for their return to Camp. He thought, *I'd walk any of those Marines into the ground.*

What I can do, he thought, *is when I turn eighteen I'll join the Army… not the Marines because I don't like seasick,* and if the others could complete that thirty mile march, I bet none of them but me would still be able to walk back the way we came rather than ride back. He chuckled at the thought. *Wouldn't that frost them if I was able to walk back.*

Relaxing into the cushions, he comforted himself with that grandiose fantasy.

From North Bend, Chris had planned to hitchhike to Ellensburg, but in preparation for the day three years from now when he would join the Army and take that forced 30 mile march, he decided to walk rather than hitchhike.

Twice, Highway Patrolmen pulled over to question him. Seeing that Chris had identification papers, money in his pocket and more than $27,000 in his bank account, they didn't bother him further. Other Highway Patrolman would then pass him by and not even slow down. *Evidently,* he thought, *those guys communicate with each other.*

Guys sometimes pulled over and offered him rides but he turned them down. It took him four and a half days to cover that 80 miles. The march up over the Snoqualmie Pass, and with a backpack, had been brutal. Even his hair hurt. He was satisfied with what he had accomplished and allowed himself to rest in the weeds for a day before tackling the steep incline up Southbound Highway 82 and then down the last 32 miles to Yakima.

At the pinnacle of the Pass, at the Rest Area, after that tough uphill climb, he took a break, peed, ate some trail food, rested, refilled his canteen, and began his walk out of the Rest Area. A woman pulled up alongside him and offered him a lift. She was ancient, probably more than 30, but still she looked very good.

His resolve to walk the rest of the way to Yakima evaporated. He threw his backpack in the back and climbed into the front seat. She offered him her hand, he took it and she said, "My name is Teena."

He said, "I'm Chris."

"Where you headed Chris?"

"Yakima,"

"You headed there to pick fruit?"

"Yup."

"You have clean clothes in that pack?"

"I do. Why'd you stop for me?"

"I passed by you before you reached the Rest Area. You have a strong walk, you're a good-looking young guy but you're sweaty, smelly, and when we get to the motel you will shower while I run your dirty clothes through the washer/dryer."

• • •

Early dawn, they awoke and went at it again. Sated, Teena said, "You have a nice body. The first time you went off almost immediately, like a firecracker, the second time was lots better, and this now is a wow. You learn fast."

Chris thought, *I've died and gone to heaven.*

"After I buy you breakfast," Teena said, "I'll drive you to where you can find work as a fruit picker. I love having sex with you. But you're younger than I realized. I'm insatiable, you're jailbait, and that's a bad combination."

• • •

He felt free. He picked apples until the apples were done, then moved on to picking cherries. When the cherries were done, and pleased to note that he had added to his account, still thinking about the trick he would pull when he joined the Army, he began the walk back down Highway 82 to where it cut back into Highway 90 and he could then head East.

Chris stopped at each Rest Area since it allowed those also having stopped to get a good look at him and check him out. He turned down all offers of lifts from guys, but at the Rest Area east of Ellensburg, Christina Howell, heading back to Eastern Washington University, slowed down her brand-new Buick and offered him a lift.

He thought, *Wow! Life away from Mom, how sweet it is.*

• • •

He took a job for a time in Missoula repairing railroad track, what was known as being a gandi dancer, until cold weather started setting in. He picked up his last paycheck, and then headed south.

CHAPTER TWO—Chris's Story

Years later, Chris, the scar-faced soldier boy, still in uniform, having a hearing aid in his left ear, was sitting on a bench in New York's Union Square Park and watching the pigeons scrambling for the grain being tossed to the ground. He mused, *I never felt more alive, more in tune with my team, than when in combat. Now I'm alone.* These pigeons are less alone than me.

He asked the old guy feeding the pidgins and sitting across from him, "There a hotel near here?

The old guy nodded, said, "I'm Harvey."

"I'm Chris."

Harvey pointed, "That's University Avenue. Two blocks down you'll find the Albert Hotel. They've got everything there, retirees, gay, straight, students, male and female prostitutes, actors, disabled vets like you and me. Everything. How much disability they give you?"

"Twenty-five percent. Sounds like my kind of place."

• • •

Two young men on the subway platform were goofing around and making others nervous when the scar-faced soldier boy, Chris Cordel, came through the turnstile. He was in uniform, had a hearing aid in his left ear, combat ribbons, a Purple Heart, and a Silver

Star pinned to his chest.

They looked at the soldier boy, he was as young as them, and assuming the soldier boy had money in his pockets—which he did—they converged. The one with the knife said, "Your money man." Soldier boy Chris Cordel grabbed with his left and turned the other's hand in a direction it wasn't supposed to turn, then dropped him with a blow to the throat. The other guy landed a punch that didn't make Chris even blink, he turned with a wolfish smile, and that was enough for the other. He took off.

One of those on the platform, a matronly-looking woman, approached Chris and said "I didn't know that the hearing impaired could stay in the military."

"Touchy subject right now. This day I received my discharge and a decent pension."

"My name is Marie Connealy, You're strong and you can handle yourself. My husband tends bar, owns a part interest in the joint. It's a rough place. Can I buy you coffee?"

"You can."

They exited the subway at the 23rd Street stop, ducked out of the cloudless cold and into a coffee shop. With coffees in front of them, Marie said, "Tell me about you?"

The soldier boy sat down his coffee cup and said, "I'm Staff Sergeant Chris Cordel now retired. It had been my plan to go into law enforcement when I left the Military. But having lost all the hearing in my right ear and half the hearing in the left without a hearing aid—law enforcement isn't hiring many deaf guys."

"You a drinker?"

"Definitely not."

"Where you staying?"

"The Albert Hotel."

"That's about four blocks from my husband's bar on Third Avenue. You ever thought about bartending?"

"Never did." In his mind's eye he replayed the scene with Colonel Scrags: *Sir! I'm either going to stay in the Army or get out to be a cop. Either way, in order to advance, I need combat experience.*

That was how he came to be transferred to Afghanistan, and ultimately, to the injuries that retired him.

• • •

It was 4 PM when Marie Connealy and Chris exited the coffee shop on 23rd Street. "This street," Marie said, "at night, becomes one of the cities favorite meeting places for the gay community. Chris, you have family?"

He thought, *how much do I want to tell her?*

"Not really. Let it lay. When I was eighteen I joined the Army. When we were finishing Basic Training, I still didn't have adult judgment, not yet anyway, but young as I was, I had more stamina, could run further, march further, was a marksman, the best in our company. When we finished our thirty-mile forced march, had eaten, and were loading up for the ride back to camp, that was when I pulled my stunt. I said, "We have to ride back? We don't get to march back?""

Colonel Flack heard this and was not amused. He said, "If you would prefer to march back Private, then feel free to do so."

"Thank you Sir." Chris then shouldered his pack and started walking. Those having observing this were still… said nothing. Jaws had dropped.

Ten miles down the road, Colonel Flack pulled up in his jeep and said, "Get in Soldier."

Chris was not feeling well, was on the verge of telling him to fuck off, Flack saw that, saw Chris struggling with it, and then say, "Yes Sir," and climb into the Jeep.

Colonel Flack chuckled, said, "You damn sure made your point Corporal."

Chris had just finished basic training and the Colonel had now promoted him to Corporal. Shortly, both Chris and his reputation would be shipped out to Korea.

• • •

Marie asked, "What did you do in Korea?"

"You're awfully nosey Marie. Mostly what I did was box, do guard duty, and run."

"That doesn't explain the scarring."

"I took a transfer to Afghanistan; I wanted combat."

"Eyes wide, Marie said, "You *wanted* combat?"

"I did. In other areas I still lacked adult judgement, but in

CHAPTER ONE—In the Beginning

Chris's gentle and almost pretty face belied his broad shoulders and toughness.

This day Chris was feeling good. He liked the routine, liked the long fast walking after being cooped up in school. No question, school was slow and boring. Others had sometimes tried to keep up with him when he made his newspaper deliveries but they couldn't long maintain his pace. Route Manager Schwin called Chris his ironman.

He had delivered his last Seattle Times Newspaper when a guy parked at the corner with his passenger door open said, "Chris Cordel."

Chris said, "Yeah, that's me. Who're you?"

"I'm Ray Cordel. I'm your father."

Stunned, Chris walked up to the car, thought on it and climbed in. His father said, "How's your mother holding up?"

"Mom has pretty well terrified our neighbors. They won't say it to her face but other kids tell me she's known as the neighborhood's wild woman. She can't seem to break the habit of getting married about every one or two years, but never to the same guy twice."

Ray Cordel nodded and said, "Yeah. First year around, same as me, they learn their lesson. When I met your mother I was young and stupid. She was awful pretty, could talk the birds out of the trees and I kidded myself that my marrying her could fix her. Evidently, I'm not that good at fixing things, not good at fixing people anyway; but I'm a damn good cop and I find out things."

"Like what?"

"Like for the last three years, from your paper route, you've been buying your own shoes, your own clothes, and you still had over $200 in your bank account. Your local shoe repairman says you're the best customer he's ever had, that you burn up more shoe leather than anyone he's ever seen."

"You said, had."

"Right. You'll be moving up. Like you," Ray said, "I'm frugal, you probably get that from me plus I've inherited. Your next bank statement will show the $27,000 I've deposited to your account. Whatever you do, don't tell your mother; hide your account, don't let her see it."

"Hah! Not likely. Why you doing this?"

"That I'm not prepared to talk about." He turned the key, started the engine, and said, "I have to go now. It was nice meeting you."

"Will I ever see you again?"

"I don't think so. I have to leave." Chris watched his father drive away and he thought, *Damn. What's wrong with me, my being all teared up like this?*

• • •

Three months later Chris learned that his father had died of pancreatic cancer. In his will, Ray Cordel had left what was in his account, less than $10,000, to his son's mother. Ritch's mother ranted, "That was just like that bastard! He left not even one penny to his own son."

"You want to give me some of it Mom?"

"That's not what your father wanted. I have to respect that."

• • •

The day after his mother's most recent marriage was the day Chris accepted the truth that if he was ever going to have a life he needed to get out, and the sooner the better. He decided he would do it after he graduated the Ninth Grade. His mother did not notice, or perhaps chose not to notice, that he had bought a backpack, a bedroll, and a road map.

Tim, his mother's latest, had sad knowing eyes, and Ray suspected that Tim had already recognized that his marriage had been a mistake.

In public, Chris's Mom played the part of the loving mother, and spoke glowingly of how proud she was of her son. In private, sometimes she was playing the role of a kind and loving mother and sometimes she was not. When not, she would say, "Chris, do you realize what my life could have been if it weren't for you? If it weren't for you I could have married the richest man in western Washington."

When his mother was half-drunk and angry she might even tell the truth, so this day Chris asked, "Mom, what ever happened to my little dog Toby?"

"I took that mangy mutt to the pound."

Walking away, Chris said over his shoulder, "Motherhood is a beautiful thing!"

• • •

On graduating the ninth grade, Tim (his Mom's Latest) gave Chris a hundred dollars while saying, "Don't tell your mother."

Chris didn't need it but the gesture moved him… seemed to uplift, make life seem worthwhile, and he had a plan.

• • •

Chris gave up his paper route on Friday. Saturday morning, knowing that the apple picking season was about to start, Chris arose early, showered, and left a note saying, 'I'm taking off for San Francisco.'

Ritch packed up a second set of clothes, caught the downtown bus, and was let off four blocks from the Greyhound Bus Terminal. He bought a ticket for the 25 mile trip to North Bend. He was heading East, not South. Easing back on the seats he reviewed in his mind the film he had seen where a Marine company had just finished their 30 mile march and were being loaded up on trucks for their return to Camp. He thought, *I'd walk any of those Marines into the ground.*

What I can do, he thought, *is when I turn eighteen I'll join the Army… not the Marines because I don't like seasick,* and if the others could complete that thirty mile march, I bet none of them but me would still be able to walk back the way we came rather than ride back. He chuckled at the thought. *Wouldn't that frost them if I was able to walk back.*

Relaxing into the cushions, he comforted himself with that grandiose fantasy.

From North Bend, Chris had planned to hitchhike to Ellensburg, but in preparation for the day three years from now when he would join the Army and take that forced 30 mile march, he decided to walk rather than hitchhike.

Twice, Highway Patrolmen pulled over to question him. Seeing that Chris had identification papers, money in his pocket and more than $27,000 in his bank account, they didn't bother him further. Other Highway Patrolman would then pass him by and not even slow down. *Evidently,* he thought, *those guys communicate with each other.*

Guys sometimes pulled over and offered him rides but he turned them down. It took him four and a half days to cover that 80 miles. The march up over the Snoqualmie Pass, and with a backpack, had been brutal. Even his hair hurt. He was satisfied with what he had accomplished and allowed himself to rest in the weeds for a day before tackling the steep incline up Southbound Highway 82 and then down the last 32 miles to Yakima.

At the pinnacle of the Pass, at the Rest Area, after that tough uphill climb, he took a break, peed, ate some trail food, rested, refilled his canteen, and began his walk out of the Rest Area. A woman pulled up alongside him and offered him a lift. She was ancient, probably more than 30, but still she looked very good.

His resolve to walk the rest of the way to Yakima evaporated. He threw his backpack in the back and climbed into the front seat. She offered him her hand, he took it and she said, "My name is Teena."

He said, "I'm Chris."

"Where you headed Chris?"

"Yakima,"

"You headed there to pick fruit?"

"Yup."

"You have clean clothes in that pack?"

"I do. Why'd you stop for me?"

"I passed by you before you reached the Rest Area. You have a strong walk, you're a good-looking young guy but you're sweaty, smelly, and when we get to the motel you will shower while I run your dirty clothes through the washer/dryer."

• • •

Early dawn, they awoke and went at it again. Sated, Teena said, "You have a nice body. The first time you went off almost immediately, like a firecracker, the second time was lots better, and this now is a wow. You learn fast."

Chris thought, *I've died and gone to heaven.*

"After I buy you breakfast," Teena said, "I'll drive you to where you can find work as a fruit picker. I love having sex with you. But you're younger than I realized. I'm insatiable, you're jailbait, and that's a bad combination."

• • •

He felt free. He picked apples until the apples were done, then moved on to picking cherries. When the cherries were done, and pleased to note that he had added to his account, still thinking about the trick he would pull when he joined the Army, he began the walk back down Highway 82 to where it cut back into Highway 90 and he could then head East.

Chris stopped at each Rest Area since it allowed those also having stopped to get a good look at him and check him out. He turned down all offers of lifts from guys, but at the Rest Area east of Ellensburg, Christina Howell, heading back to Eastern Washington University, slowed down her brand-new Buick and offered him a lift.

He thought, *Wow! Life away from Mom, how sweet it is.*

• • •

He took a job for a time in Missoula repairing railroad track, what was known as being a gandi dancer, until cold weather started setting in. He picked up his last paycheck, and then headed south.

CHAPTER TWO—Chris's Story

Years later, Chris, the scar-faced soldier boy, still in uniform, having a hearing aid in his left ear, was sitting on a bench in New York's Union Square Park and watching the pigeons scrambling for the grain being tossed to the ground. He mused, *I never felt more alive, more in tune with my team, than when in combat. Now I'm alone.* These pigeons are less alone than me.

He asked the old guy feeding the pidgins and sitting across from him, "There a hotel near here?

The old guy nodded, said, "I'm Harvey."

"I'm Chris."

Harvey pointed, "That's University Avenue. Two blocks down you'll find the Albert Hotel. They've got everything there, retirees, gay, straight, students, male and female prostitutes, actors, disabled vets like you and me. Everything. How much disability they give you?"

"Twenty-five percent. Sounds like my kind of place."

• • •

Two young men on the subway platform were goofing around and making others nervous when the scar-faced soldier boy, Chris Cordel, came through the turnstile. He was in uniform, had a hearing aid in his left ear, combat ribbons, a Purple Heart, and a Silver

Star pinned to his chest.

They looked at the soldier boy, he was as young as them, and assuming the soldier boy had money in his pockets—which he did—they converged. The one with the knife said, "Your money man." Soldier boy Chris Cordel grabbed with his left and turned the other's hand in a direction it wasn't supposed to turn, then dropped him with a blow to the throat. The other guy landed a punch that didn't make Chris even blink, he turned with a wolfish smile, and that was enough for the other. He took off.

One of those on the platform, a matronly-looking woman, approached Chris and said "I didn't know that the hearing impaired could stay in the military."

"Touchy subject right now. This day I received my discharge and a decent pension."

"My name is Marie Connealy, You're strong and you can handle yourself. My husband tends bar, owns a part interest in the joint. It's a rough place. Can I buy you coffee?"

"You can."

They exited the subway at the 23rd Street stop, ducked out of the cloudless cold and into a coffee shop. With coffees in front of them, Marie said, "Tell me about you?"

The soldier boy sat down his coffee cup and said, "I'm Staff Sergeant Chris Cordel now retired. It had been my plan to go into law enforcement when I left the Military. But having lost all the hearing in my right ear and half the hearing in the left without a hearing aid—law enforcement isn't hiring many deaf guys."

"You a drinker?"

"Definitely not."

"Where you staying?"

"The Albert Hotel."

"That's about four blocks from my husband's bar on Third Avenue. You ever thought about bartending?"

"Never did." In his mind's eye he replayed the scene with Colonel Scrags: *Sir! I'm either going to stay in the Army or get out to be a cop. Either way, in order to advance, I need combat experience.*

That was how he came to be transferred to Afghanistan, and ultimately, to the injuries that retired him.

• • •

It was 4 PM when Marie Connealy and Chris exited the coffee shop on 23rd Street. "This street," Marie said, "at night, becomes one of the cities favorite meeting places for the gay community. Chris, you have family?"

He thought, *how much do I want to tell her?*

"Not really. Let it lay. When I was eighteen I joined the Army. When we were finishing Basic Training, I still didn't have adult judgment, not yet anyway, but young as I was, I had more stamina, could run further, march further, was a marksman, the best in our company. When we finished our thirty-mile forced march, had eaten, and were loading up for the ride back to camp, that was when I pulled my stunt. I said, "We have to ride back? We don't get to march back?"

Colonel Flack heard this and was not amused. He said, "If you would prefer to march back Private, then feel free to do so."

"Thank you Sir." Chris then shouldered his pack and started walking. Those having observing this were still… said nothing. Jaws had dropped.

Ten miles down the road, Colonel Flack pulled up in his jeep and said, "Get in Soldier."

Chris was not feeling well, was on the verge of telling him to fuck off, Flack saw that, saw Chris struggling with it, and then say, "Yes Sir," and climb into the Jeep.

Colonel Flack chuckled, said, "You damn sure made your point Corporal."

Chris had just finished basic training and the Colonel had now promoted him to Corporal. Shortly, both Chris and his reputation would be shipped out to Korea.

• • •

Marie asked, "What did you do in Korea?"

"You're awfully nosey Marie. Mostly what I did was box, do guard duty, and run."

"That doesn't explain the scarring."

"I took a transfer to Afghanistan; I wanted combat."

"Eyes wide, Marie said, "You *wanted* combat?"

"I did. In other areas I still lacked adult judgement, but in combat it turned out I was a natural, I came into my own, came into being a warrior."

Chris, looking at Marie, thought back to the day he learned his mother had died in what appeared to be a vehicular suicide. A sad day. *After all* he thought, *she was my mother.* He was sad—and surprised that h**e** cared. Also, he was surprised. He had assumed that his Mom would probably be the last one standing.

• • •

The bar was a low-class hookers bar. Most of the hookers were black, and Marie's husband Pat took Chris on as a trainee bartender. Turned out he was good at it—plus he could handle himself. Chis and Pat were on duty behind the bar when pro football player Chuck Meadows, clearly under the influence, entered the bar. Why? This was a well-paid pro athlete, not a bottom feeder, so why was he here in a low-class hooker's bar? The thing was that he was looking for a chance to kick some ass.

Chris Cordel slipped the hearing aid into his pocket, came out from behind the bar and asked, 'Why you here?"

Meadows, the larger man, threw a punch Chris parried while returning a punch that was a blur. The enlarged first two knuckles of his fist sank into Meadows chest below his heart. Meadows gasp was followed by the sound of the knife-edge of Chris's other hand cracking across his Adam's apple.

Meadows went down and Pat was already on the phone and calling the cops.

• • •

Dawn Tyler had heard the story of Meadows getting his clock cleaned and saw a bumper sticker that said, Shit Happens. She said to herself, *got that right*, and went looking for Chris Cordel. It took awhile, but she found out who Chris Cordel was, how he had cleaned up on Chuck Meadows, and she was sitting in the parked car with gay coworker Alfie while the two of them watched as Chris came walking down University Avenue from 14th Street. Alfie muttered, "Uh huh. Square chin, blue eyes, and look at that basket."

"Alfie," Dawn said, "You are terrible."

"I know. I expected to see a bigger man. His being desirable yet dangerous makes him irresistible."

"You may not be his type Alfie?"

"That'd be his loss since I shake a pretty mean box. Dawn, you don't know… he may have a dark side so you be careful… and then you tell me everything."

• • •

Dawn Tyler accosted Chris in the lobby of the Alberton Hotel. She blurted, "I follow sports. You move like a boxer."

"I started as a boxer, then, in Phoenix, I took training in unarmed combat before joining the Army." He thought, *what does she want? Why is she in my face?*

"You have scarring on your face. Were you in combat?"

"Why you asking?"

She swallowed. "We need help. We're desperate. It's hard. I work in the garment district. We have Abel Strauss, the boss's son. He grabs tits, grabs crotch. Those that complain get fired. Some of the girls put up with it because they really need the job."

Chris thought on it, muttered an "Uh huh," and said, "You have a picture of him?"

• • •

Abel Strauss was followed onto the elevator in the Strauss Building by someone he thought was a black man with a scarred face, long straight black hair, dark shades, not wearing a hearing aid, and wearing dark gloves. The supposed black man grabbed Abel's right wrist, turned it over, slammed it against the wall, and four hard punches to the back of his hand left small bones and tendons damaged. Abel was screaming in pain and fear while the hand ballooned up and turned purple.

Detective Mathers investigated the assault. He visited the Strauss Foundation, made inquiries, and one of those queried asked, "Which hand was mashed?"

"The right hand."

"Hah!" one woman said, "Now he'll have to do his ass, crotch, and tit-grabbing with his left hand." Detective Mathers, hearing this, was no fan of vigilante justice, but then, he did have two young daughters. His eyes lit up, he nodded, and his investigation of this crime slowed to a halt as he concentrated on more urgent cases. Justice being served, Abel, being intolerant of discomfort, developed an addiction to opiates.

• • •

Dawn paid Chris another visit. "Abel's back at work now; he looks fearful, and all we have to do is say something about our big black boyfriend and he beats a retreat.

Chris lived with a hotplate, and had his stew on simmer. "I have little patience with cooking so each time I cook I make enough stew for two or three meals."

He set her up with a bowl of stew, and to be polite, she ate it all… and that had not been easy. Then she said, "How did you season this stew?"

"I slice up my vegetables, my polish sausage, bring them to a boil and add a can of Campbell's Clam Chowder for seasoning."

"Obviously, you have limits. If anyone ever offers to move in with you then you will need to let them do the cooking."

CHAPTER THREE—Cowboy Bob

In the Los Angeles Police Headquarters, lab tech Nancy Poletti rushed back to her office, hands full, dropped her pen, and accidentally kicked it under the desk. She was scrabbling under the desk for her pen when Commissioner Hogan, plus an officer Poletti did not see, entered. Thinking the office empty, Hogan said, "He's never going to make it to Court. That's being taken care of right now." They had turned to leave when Poletti's head bumped up. Hogan paused, "Did you hear that?" Hogan walked around the desk, looked down at Poletti's butt and said, "Come on out Poletti."

She scrabbled back out. "Poletti," Commissioner Hogan said, "You never heard a damn thing did you?"

"No Sir. Not one damn word."

"That's good Poletti, that's very good. We're all on the same team; we protect each other. You remember that."

"Yes sir, we're all on the same team, I remember, I surely do remember that. The same team."

• • •

Nancy Poletti did not own a car. Still, she entered the parking garage, walked down the ramp and out of the building, entered the bank, emptied her account and taxied to the airport. Seeing that a flight to Chicago would be loading, she bought a ticket.

When she landed in Chicago she left her cellphone in the rest room, caught a ride into the city, and took the Greyhound to New York.

• • •

At one of the rest stops Nancy had time, bought a new cellphone, and made her call. Dawn Tyler was there to meet her when she exited the buss.

"Dawn, I ran for my life."

"I have some clothes that will fit you. I'm going to put you up with someone; he is unbelievably dangerous to others, not to you, and he will protect you, but his cooking is terrible."

"Sounds like a fun guy."

"He's intense and I don't think he even knows what fun is."

• • •

Dawn called Detective Mathers. When he met with them, Nancy told him what she knew.

He said, "What is it you want?"

"I want Commissioner Hogan held accountable for what he's done, and I want my old life back."

"Nancy, you knowing this about Hogan, whether or not Hogan is indicted, your old life is over. You dare not go through regular police channels. Not yet anyway. If you do, Hogan and friends will know and you're dead. What you can do is write a letter to the FBI detailing everything and stating that you will come forward only if and when Hogan is indicted. Have someone wearing gloves travel to Chicago and mail the letter from there to the FBI Office in DC. Anything come up, you call me. I'll get in touch if I hear anything."

Dawn took Nancy's letter to the Chicago Post Office, bought a stamp, put it on the letter, and dropped it off at the Chicago Post Office. Then she returned to New York.

It took a while, but now knowing where to look, the FBI gathered enough information to indict Commissioner Hogan. While they had enough to indict, without Nancy's testimony, possibly not enough to convict.

• • •

Chris, after the shrapnel wounds, and having been awarded the Silver Star and had been promoted to Staff Sergeant, had turned down a transfer back to the States, and had requested a transfer to the Military Police. Then an explosion took out his hearing. As a civilian, he was licensed to bear arms, and was an excellent marksman. Still, all his applications for employment as a policeman had been turned down. The fact that the government had awarded him a disability rating had more than something to do with this.

Two gentlemen, saying they were FBI, showed up at Chris's door. Carefully, he checked their ID's. One of them said, "What if our ID's hadn't checked out?"

Chris looked him in the eye. "You'd be dead."

Agent Levin's eyes narrowed while Morrow, the older of the Agents, nodded and exclaimed, "Jesus! You mean it. You are one serious fucking dude. You actually think you could take down two FBI?"

"There might be collateral damage, but I would survive. If you weren't FBI, not so hard."

"Nancy Poletti told us that she wants you, Chris Cordel, as well as the two of us, to escort her back to LA."

Agent Levin said, "I asked her why she wants you and she said, 'because he's tough, he's smart, and I'm comfortable sleeping in the same room, the same bed with him, and I can't do that with either of you guys.'"

Chris eased into a cooperative alliance with the two FBI, they worked well together and few words were necessary as they provided Poletti with round the clock protection.

• • •

The three of them escorted Nancy into the Courtroom. Commissioner Hogan, on seeing Nancy's arrival in Court, and with her having Security, Hogan's face sagged. He huddled with his attorneys, they cut a deal, and for his testimony against the others, Hogan received a sentence of twenty to life in a Federal Prison.

The very air in LA now felt hostile to Nancy. She and Chris returned to New York, she moved in with Chris and took over the cooking. Dawn still checked in from time to time, but less so as time passed. "Chris," Nancy said, I don't want to ever again see the inside of a Police Station. So, other than the cooking, which you should be grateful I'm willing to take over, what can I do?"

"Nancy, you are the most verbal chick I ever met, you have a quirky personality and you could study, go to school, take dance lessons, take up acting—you could end up as the lab tech on one of those TV cop shows. Whatever you want, go for it. And you could stay here.

I have money. My father was a cop and I only saw him that one time. That's why I want to be a cop, that way I can get to know him better. I want to hold onto that connection with my father. My dad provided me with a bundle of cash, I piled up a little more overseas and I'm earning more than enough to support the two of us, almost double that, and I get a check from the Government every month. So you take your time; there's no rush for you to do anything."

"Chris, You're nice to me and sometimes you remind me of the cops I once knew. You know everything about me and I don't know anything about you. I'm confused. How can this be?"

Chris wagged his head. "What I'm doing now, it's okay I guess—but I want more—since that day when I met my father I've wanted to do police work, either in the Army or in the civilian world. Look around. I live frugally, work out every morning. I seldom watch TV, I read, and earn almost double what I spend. Even having you, which is nice, I'm incomplete."

"I'm not enough?"

"Not being a cop is what's not enough."

• • •

In November, Nancy took up classes in acting and dance. She then signed up for an apprenticeship in Summer Stock at the Pottsdam Playhouse in upstate New York. "I would like it," she said, "if for those ten weeks, eight shows, you would come up once a week and fuck my brains out."

"Count on it."

• • •

Chris received a call. Nancy said, "Chris, we have a situation and we need you."

He drove up, parked alongside the Playhouse, and walked around to where the apprentices were busy painting flats. Nancy saw him, ran up and kissed him.

Everyone was smiling, being cheerful and joking, but he could feel it—he thought, *Jesus, it's like before going into battle. You get jumpy and could cut the tension with a knife!* Something is definitely wrong.

"Nancy, what's going on?"

"I'll tell you when we break for dinner. Meanwhile, you could move the flats that have been painted around to the back and lean them against the building to dry."

A hulking young man, taking his time as he assembled a flat, said to a female apprentice who was no more than fourteen, "Don't worry, you get your virginity back after six weeks."

Seeing the look on Chris's face, Nancy grabbed his arm. He thought, *Uh huh. He's the what that's going on.*

The set designer, a fussy and smallish man, was genuinely pleased with the set work being done—and yet he looked tense. When the company broke for their evening meal, Nancy held back, let the others get ahead of them, and then they were joined by the actor and Director Harry Praaste. They crossed the blacktopped road and walking up the dirt road to the barn converted to a kitchen and dining room.

Director Praaste said, "This Playhouse was owned and run by our present producer's former husband. He never once let her on stage. She received this property as part of their divorce settlement and then she became its producer and star. Then she saw this Cowboy Bob character, who, except for the New York accent, he even looks a little like John Wayne. She saw him as a natural and believed she'd discovered the next John Wayne.

"You just heard him," Nancy said, "remark that young girls will get their virginity back in six weeks… he's making threat's, saying, 'They brought me in to play Cowboy Bob, and that's what I'm going to do. I'm Cowboy Bob.'"

• • •

The meal was not eaten in silence. There was nervous laughter and giggling in the air that did not mask the tension. Clearly, they sensed something was about to happen.

Meal complete, Director Praaste said, "Company, we have to meet with Cowboy Bob. We would like the rest of you to leave." They did—even kitchen staff.

Praaste handed Cowboy Bob a document and said, "You've now been served with a restraining order, along with a return ticket to the city, barring you from these premises." Chis had put his hearing aid in his pocket.

Praaste stepped back. Cowboy Bob arose and rushed. His foot was still in the air and sweeping forward when Chris caught it with his own foot and swept it aside. Cowboy crashed down hard. He arose and went for the serving knife. "Praaste," Chris said, "I don't *need* you so get out of here. *NOW!*"

• • •

Cowboy Bob advanced cautiously with the knife. Chris round-kicked his front knee on it's side, first with his right, and Cowboy Bob was frozen, couldn't move. Chris then round-kicked the knee on its other side with his left foot. Cowboy's face drained of blood and he dropped the knife. Chris was not through, was disgusted, and wanted Cowboy Bob to know more pain. He delivered two blistering blows to Cowboy Bob's sternum.

Two Police cars arrived, the cops were efficient, called for medical backup, and took statements from everyone.

Chris showed the two Officers his gun permit, said, "if I'd had my gun I probably would have shot the son-of-a-bitch, but then I would have had to fill out reports, hang out around here for days, and I have a job I need to get back to in the city. It's a good thing for him I didn't have my gun."

CHAPTER FOUR—Quantico

The company put on eight shows in eight weeks—Nancy was in five of the shows and had a major role in three of them. She stayed focused no matter what mishap did or did not occur onstage. Chris witnessed the occasion when, in a support role, she was onstage with the star when he lost his lines. Nancy's quirky ad libs, her humor and personality rescued the scene—got it back on track, and she received very decent reviews and many thanks from the lead actor.

"Nancy," Chris said, "I have a knack for dealing with physical threat, I was born with it, and like you, I work damn hard keeping that talent tuned up. You have talent, you work hard, we have that in common, but what's different is that I don't have to go looking for physical threat, it comes to me and I'm ready when it comes calling."

"What are you saying?"

"I suspect you returned to your acting and dance classes, not only to hone your skills, but also to hide from making the rounds and getting turned down as an actor. Maybe I'm doing the same thing—hiding from the fact that nobody wants me as a policeman. Trouble comes looking for me, but no stage or TV producer is going to come looking for you, which, leaving you here with me, suits me just fine. I like having you here, but is this what you want?"

"I'm good. I have talent!"

"Agreed. And therefore, without much effort, you can get parts in going nowhere shows, pick up a pile of credits, lead a casual and comfortable life here with me, something I'd like, or you can have a career. It puzzles me… I'm not clear on whether you're willing to take that extra step."

• • •

That Fall Nancy received good reviews in a decent little play —a play that ran for 17 performances and was never heard from again. She said, "Chris, enough of this. I want Matty Helms for my agent, he has clients on all the networks, but I can't get past his front desk."

Chris thought on it. Then he scouted it out. He said, "Matty is a nervous, jumpy type guy. He leaves his office promptly at 5 PM. Catch him when he comes out and is heading for the elevator."

Four days in a row, Nancy was waiting for him when he exited his office. Friday, he peeked out of his office, heaved a sigh of relief on seeing she was not there, rushed out and hit the elevator button. When the doors opened, he entered—and Nancy was waiting in the elevator.

That night, when the bar closed and Chris returned to the Alberton, Nancy was waiting, leaped into his arms and said, "Matty Helms is now my Agent."

• • •

On stage, on TV, Nancy worked all the time. Big parts, little parts, it didn't matter, she worked. Eighteen months after signing with the Helms Agency, Nancy Poletti signed a contract as the quirky lab tech in a new cop show and the new show became her new relationship.

Chris and Nancy were drifting apart. They were friends—frequent lovers—but friends going in different directions business-wise, personal-wise, and geographically. Chris helped her move into her own apartment, and said, "I'll miss your cooking. Damn! I'll miss your cooking." She kissed him and said, "You and Dawn Tyler are my two best friends. I wish the two of you could get together."

"I like her too. She's one of my favorite people but it wouldn't work."

• • •

"Chris" Dawn said, "I want out of Strauss and Company."

"Why?"

"The company is in process of falling apart. Drug dealers receive as warm a reception as prospective buyers. I don't want to be a party to this meltdown. But what about you? I don't think you've taken off more than five days in the last six months."

"You're right. I let off steam with my morning workouts but I've been doing this more than five years, and it's time for me to do something else. The VA Doctors believe that possibly, with surgery, there is a chance they may be able to restore the hearing in my right ear. So, what've I got to lose?"

"What about the left ear?"

"I won't take a chance with the hearing I have in that ear even if the right ear surgery works."

· · ·

When Chris awoke, it was night. He was in a hospital bed and could hear the rain beating on the window. He covered his left ear tight with his hand—and he could still hear the rain—his eyes teared, something they hadn't done since he was a boy, and he thought, *when I quite this hospital bed, I'm going to boll weevil my way into the FBI.*

· · ·

Agents Levin and Morrow reported to the Field Office of Supervisor Orvis. "The two of you," Orvis said, "along with civilian Chris Cordel, rode shotgun on Nancy Poletti to testify in the Hogan case. What was your impression of this man? Would you feel safe having this man guarding your back?"

Levin said, "I would. He is a decorated war veteran and has all his hearing back in his right ear. Even before that he was tough, smart, and there is no back down in him."

Supervisor Orvis looked up at the ceiling and slowly shook his head. "I was afraid you'd say something like that. Agent Morrow, would you agree with that assessment?"

"I would. He doesn't have much formal education but he's well read, smart, and a true warrior."

"God, how I hate being told I'm wrong. When I read this man's resume and saw that for the past five years he has been bartending in a hookers bar, I thought, this man is a sociopath, a deviant, and no way do we want this man in the FBI."

Levin and Morrow looked at each other. Morrow said, "He may be a sociopath, a deviant, I don't know about that, but he's smart, alert, sees everything, is battle tested, and he can handle himself."

"I checked," Orvis said, "With Nancy Poletti. She said: "I trust this man, and whatever shortcomings he may have, he delivers."

"Then," Orvis said, "I checked his service jacket—did you know this man is the recipient of two Purple Heart and the Silver Star? No? Plus, he has a reputation as a man who squeezes a nickel until the buffalo cries."

Morrow and Levin looked at each other and nodded. "That's no surprise," Morrow said, "His crummy corner hotel room, except for the books, looks like a dog kennel. Austerity would be a polite word for it."

"So," Levin said, "what will you do."

"Despite the limited hearing in his left ear, I will recommend that we accept this man in the training program at Quantico."

• • •

Wayne Deckley's Quantico Assessment stated:

Trainee Chris Cordel is a decorated combat soldier, and in our training exercises, he demonstrated good judgement and quickly. His hand to hand combat skills, plus his hand speed, are exceptional. He clearly has more stamina than any other trainee I have ever seen. He is an expert marksman while his service record gives evidence of alertness and judgement under fire. He has no family, his formal education ended in the ninth grade, and he compensates for this by being an omnivorous reader including psychology, history, and law books—he is well-acquainted with the law.

Trainee Cordel works well with female trainees and they trust him.

Training Supervisor Wayne Deckley

CHAPTER FIVE—Chris Gets Blackballed

Newly appointed FBI Director Harry Holbrook called in his Senior Personnel Officer. "Agent Tracy, I have received a report that amongst those who served with Trainee Chris Cordel in Afghanistan, there are those who claim he is a psychotic killing machine. Then, reviewing Personnel files, I see that while Agent Chris Cordel has an exemplary record within the Bureau—how can this be, what are we missing?

This is a man raised by a mother who was married seven times and then committed vehicular suicide. His father was a Police Officer who he met only once shortly before the father died of pancreatic cancer.

Agent Chris Cordel is a man who does not sleep well, has nightmares, and I strongly suspect he will one day explode. I know that of which I speak, my having lived this firsthand. We owe him for the service he has delivered and therefore he will be allowed to submit a Letter of Resignation. That will forego the indignity of his being terminated, his weapon will be retrieved, and his right to own or bear arms will be rescinded.

This meeting is adjourned."

• • •

Chris received a visit from Charley Justice, his senior partner.

Charley reported it all and said, "Chris, I'm devastated. You need to submit a Letter of Resignation, otherwise you will be getting the ax. They will confiscate your weapon and they'll be serving you with an order denying you the right to own and bear arms."

Chris was still, dumbfounded. Then he nodded and said, "What about you Charley? What's going to happen with you?"

"Me? In my reports I pointed out you were a damn good Agent and I'll be tarred with the same brush— I'll survive—but what about you?"

"Charley, I have a little money, more than a little, and me and my money are going to disappear. They'll have a hard time serving me with anything. Charley, thanks for the heads up, it was good working with you."

"Same here."

• • •

A Certified letter was in the mail.

To the FBI,

I, Agent Chris Cordel, being troubled by problems I see developing within the FBI, am now taking a Leave of Absence to resolve the question of whether I will choose to remain with the FBI. You will hear from me when I come to a decision.

Respectfully, Agent Chris Cordel

• • •

Chris flew from New York to Tucson, looked through the want ads, found a clunker of a car that obviously would *not* pass the emission test, and paid cash for it. He registered the Title at the Department of Motor Vehicles. Then drove to the Courthouse in Tucson, parked the car with the windows open, left the car keys on the passenger seat, and exited the car with a pint of Sunny Jim in his hand. He left the Sunny Jim sitting on a bench in the bus station, took the bus to Phoenix, and from there he booked a flight to San Francisco.

From there he took the Greyhound to Seattle.

• • •

About the last place to look for a man with money would be at the Seattle Community College. Chris Cordel was taking classes in English Literature and Psychology; he found those subjects interesting.

Fall Quarter, the drizzle of a steady rainfall began, and Lucy Ballard, threadbare, was in his English Literature class. She was sixteen and living with two other female students in a tiny apartment. The three of them had to count every penny.

"Chris," Lucy said, "I don't get it, why are we doing our classwork together? Why are you focused on me? Despite the scars, you're still a good-looking guy in your twenties, you have money, while I'm as poor as a church mouse. I'm cute as hell, but I'm only 5 foot tall and just turned 16. From the inside this doesn't feel creepy, but from the outside, I'm told, it looks like it could get creepy real fast."

Chris nodded. "Lucy, I wouldn't have let it get creepy, but now, as Shakespeare's character Jacques would say, 'Let us become better strangers.'"

And they did.

• • •

Chris was spending time in a hookers bar on Twelfth and Jackson. It reminded him of the hooker's bar where he had tended bar for five years; the only difference being that most of the clientele in the bar, almost all, were black.

Anna Stern, a good looking light brown girl, bellied up next to him and declared, "You're a cop."

"Was. I'm an ex-military cop. When I lost the hearing in my right ear and half of it in my left ear, that's when I stopped being a cop. "

" Like I said, you're a cop."

"You can fuck off any time."

Leaving the bar, Chris thought, she's young, five feet four inches tall, nice face, good body, comes across as tough, smart, I think she's a drinker, could be into drugs. She's a survivor rather than a winner. *What surprises me is that I like her.*

• • •

Richie Gross, was bobbing his head and grinning while keeping time with the sound of a song only he could hear. He was carrying a slender four foot long object wrapped in a beach towel as he entered the building.

Chris had entered the building and was looking at the bulletin board when the screaming started. When screaming or shooting starts, civilians run away while cops run towards. Chris ran towards.

Richie was wielding a Samurai sword, had already butchered three, and was advancing on Lucy Ballard who was cornered. Chris threw one of his two books—the one on English Literature—it hit Richie in the back of the neck, and Chris shouted, *"Hey Asshole! I'm coming for you!"* Having the other book in his left hand, the sword cut through the spine of the book, then took it out of his hand, and then cut halfway down into Chris's hand. Chris hit Richie with his right fist and dropped him like a stone. Later, Chris would claim that his having banged Richie's head on the floor and having given him a subdural hematoma had been an accident. He looked to Richie's three victims. Two had bled out. Lucy had returned and took the third victim in her arms and held and rocked her until she was gone. Lucy was crying and still holding her even though the girl had bled out.

Meanwhile, Chris had flipped Richie on his face, had trapped the swordsman's right hand up high on his back, while his own left hand was compressed tight up in his own right armpit. Still, he was leaking blood. Richie was moaning his way back into consciousness and Chris was not being gentle with him.

Two Policemen with drawn weapons charged in. Chris looked up. "My ID is in my left rear pocket. Don't blow my cover."

The Cop lifted his ID, saw that he was FBI and said, "You taking him on unarmed makes you either the bravest man I ever met or else you're just plain nuts!"

To himself, Chris said, *The student is gone. The warrior is back!*

• • •

Two RN's arrived with a rolling stretcher. One of them said, "You've lost a lot of blood, you're in shock so don't even try to move." They loaded him on the stretcher and with siren screaming, delivered him to nearby Harborview Hospital. In cases this serious, they do not undress the patient; they cut them out of their clothes and then gown them.

• • •

The hand had been examined, x-rayed, and Chris was loaded up on pain killers when Doctor Bozeman said, "Chris, The first two fingers, the little finger, and thumb show little damage. I may be able to tie things up so the first, second, and even the little finger will be functional, but there's not much I can do with that third finger, the knuckle is split all to hell and it would be more cosmetic than useful."

"Doc," Chris said, "I need that hand being functional. If the third finger is going to get in my way then get rid of it! I don't need pretty but I do need functional."

• • •

FBI Director Harry Holbrook was in Seattle and on-scene within hours and sat in while Seattle Police took reports from everyone and especially, he listened to Lucy Ballard's report.

Chris had never seen Director Holbrook except in photos. From his hospital bed he looked up, recognized the Director and his mood was sour. "You here to officially kick me off the FBI?"

"After you did this? I couldn't even if I wanted to, and I don't want to. Besides, I looked further, I should say deeper. You developed some political enemies in Afghanistan and they'd poisoned the air with the rumor that you're a psychotic killer."

"That what gave you the hard-on to get rid of me?"

"Tough question. That's part of it. Doctor Bozeman tells me that if you hadn't had that book in your hand you would have lost most of your hand leaving only your little finger."

"I made a mistake. Rather than sweeping the sword aside I blocked up on it. That was a serious mistake. I don't often make that kind of a mistake. That kind of mistake can be fatal; won't be doing that again."

• • •

When Chris awoke he was in a hospital bed and Director Holbrook was staring out the window and out across the Puget Sound.

Hearing Chris moan, Holbrook turned and said, "How you feeling?"

"Like crap, woozy, how'd the surgery go?"

"That took more than two hours, tying things up, putting the hand back together. The third finger's gone. You are now on a month's medical leave of absence with pay, plus there's the back pay you never collected. When your left hand gets functional we'll put you on light duties until you get strength back in your hand."

"I'm still woozy, so maybe I already asked, but why did you have such a hard-on to get rid of me?"

"You didn't ask. My father was a decorated Police Officer. But also, he was a sadist, an alcoholic, and regularly beat the crap out of me and my Mom. He committed suicide, same as your mom. That trick you pulled—getting that poor slob in Tucson to steal your car—we had him on the hot seat for days insisting that he tell us where he'd hid your body. He was a two-bit guy, a shoplifter and purse-snatcher. And here we were accusing him of murdering an FBI Agent and hiding his body—I have to admit he blubbered good. Setting him up like that was sadistic."

"I suppose so, but it was also, the way you tell it, it's kind of funny."

"You're a warrior Chris, and you're now back in the good graces of the FBI."

• • •

Ritch was awarded a second monthly disability check.

• • •

Two weeks later Chris had returned and was sitting at the bar when Anna Stern entered. Big eyed, she stared at him, stared at his hand.

The eyes of the tall black guy in the pork pie hat were not turned in Chris's direction, but he walked back and forth, watching Chris out of the corner of his eye. He walked up. "Only two kinds of white guys come in this bar, cops and tricks. You're FBI so you not here to bust street hookers, you no trick, so why you here?"

Chris had taken a small, soft rubber ball out of his pocket and was squeezing it with his first two finger and left thumb. He said,

"Change of scenery maybe. Some things I do, I don't always know why."

"You talking in riddles man. I read about you. You was unarmed but you took down a guy swinging a Japanese sword. One cop called you Mad Dog, said: If Mad Dog comes for you, bullets, swords, nothing's going to stop him and he'll get you, Damn! I'm bad, but you must be the baddest dude around."

"What they call you?"

"Charley. Last time you was here, that was my sister you told to fuck off. Now she's standing at the other end of the bar and looking at you all bug-eyed."

"I saw. Want to tell me about you Charley?"

"About me? Not much to tell. My little sister Anna and me, we been on the street since she was 13, me close up on 15… why I telling you this? Mostly, I keeps my head down, do a little dealing, small time things, some protection. My little sister, she kicked drugs, drinks too much, been hooking since she was 13, I'd like to get her out of this life, I think she could, I can't . . .."

"Maybe, or maybe not." Chris shrugged. "I'm not into judging you."

Charley looked at him sharp-eyed, then nodded.

• • •

Four days later, Chris met with Charley and Anna Stern. He said, "Anna, right now, I have a lot of pull at Seattle Community College. I talked to Administrator Watson about you, told her you have the face and expression of an angel, but under all that, you're one angry mean black chick, still, supposedly, you're one of those righteous hookers that doesn't rip off tricks. I told Watson you've been living on the streets since you were thirteen and you'd never overcome that.

"Dora Davis is one of those Social Worker types and got pissed at me for saying that. She said, 'She could be one of those, given half a chance, could turn her life around and make something of her life.'"

"So," Charley said, "what did you say?"

"I said Seattle Community College owes me and I could get her a scholarship but what would be the point? She'd be gone in less than a week. Dora Davis argued with me on that— so just to prove my point I got your sister the damn Scholarship."

Anna was fuming, but she said nothing, tried not to let it show, but not very hard.

"To prove my point, I set your sister up for a two-year scholarship program and on Friday your sister will have to make a choice. Registration begins at One PM on Friday. I'll be there and to prove my point I'll be offering your sister two hundred dollars not to accept the Scholarship."

· · ·

Chris was a decent actor. Friday, he managed to look surprised when Anna registered. Through gritted teeth she said, "You know what Chris, I should have taken the two hundred first and then took the Scholarship. I hate your white pig guts and that's why I took the scholarship and you can shove them hundreds up your lily-white ass!"

· · ·

Chris flew back to DC. On the flight, he thought, *Anna, you won't be seeing me again unless you actually make it through. But if the day ever comes when you get your degree, that day I'll be there."*

CHAPTER SIX—Lucy Ballard Returns

Chucky Dusay had been drunk for six years, but it wasn't working. He didn't have the language to describe it, but no matter how much he drank, moments of absolute lucidity kept creeping in and he remembered and felt the pain. He thought, *Time to give it up.*

He sobered up, but sober he still remembered, could not always deny the pain. One of the ways he relieved the pain was killing people and then leaving notes that said: "Catch me if you can."

A meeting of Agents working the Catch Me Case gathered at Quantico. Nine Senior Agents presented the facts and the impressions they had gathered in their respective cases.

Charles Mifflin, the Chair of the Meeting, arose and said, "I want to thank each of our Case Presenters. Now I would like to hear from others." Looking to the back of the room, he said, "Let's start with you Agent Cordel. You've just returned to duty, we don't know you, and we're all abuzz, curious about you. You've heard the case for the first time, so tell us what you're hearing and then maybe we'll know a little more about you."

Chris cleared his throat, didn't rise, but his voice rang clear. "Putting me on the spot are you? What I'm hearing is that Catch Me is someone who grew up in an unstable environment, is a well-organized psychopath, is not educated, but is intelligent, and able to blend in. Everyone agrees on that point. These crimes have been committed in areas as varied as Atascadero and Portland, Main. Some have speculated he is involved in some facet of the transportation industry. Every one of these offenses has been committed within a few miles of a railroad yard and I agree with those who believe he is an itinerant, a tramp, he commits his crimes and catches the next freight out of town. In cold weather he heads south. When it warms up he heads north. The methods he uses to dispatch his victim are varied, he has dispatched nine we know of, has left notes on each of those times we know of, lending credence to the thought that he fancies himself as a pretty smart guy who is taunting us— and that's where I part company with many of you—I don't think so.

"I believe our Catch Me Killer's early years were in an unstable environment and he survived by moving on. Even having acquired a decent job and having the prospect of a decent relationship, at the first hint of instability he moves on. He's a psychopath and psychopaths either blend in, or like Charles Manson or Hitler, will develop a following. This guy's a loner and keeps moving on. I suspect that the only stable environment he's ever known is prison. The message he leaves: Catch Me if You Can, while it sounds like braggadocio, I don't think it is, I think it's his plea, and at the same time his own self-denial, that he hungers for a return to the only stable environment he's ever known, the three hots and a cot and the stability that prison life affords. That's why he leaves messages saying, 'Catch Me If You Can.'

When you do catch him, and you will, since he unknowingly wants to get caught, he will be quick, even relieved, to confess his crimes. I think you will catch him while he's headed to or from the freight-yard. That's all I have to say.'"

In the silence that followed, Mifflin said, "This much I did not expect from you—Anyone else have something to say?"

They did not.

When they did catch Charley Dusay, he was quick to say, "Okay! You got me. I killed them all."

• • •

A year later, Chris was staring across the Potomac when his cellphone rang. It was FBI Director Harry Holbrook. "Cordel, you've been on the ground and working cases since Seattle, I've been watching—we've all been watching. You're as good on the ground as any Agent we have."

Chris looked again across the Potomac. "You think?"

"I will not concede you could be the best, but I will concede that you're in damn good company. You may be our best in a firefight. Meet with me in my office.

"Agent Cordel, I would like you to go undercover. We have three murder cases in Arizona. Each of the victims were guys having ties with the Bondage/Discipline Community." Arizona Police don't have much experience with that population, the BD&SM community seems to be more law abiding than the larger community, and Detective Woody Aldridge wants someone who can go in undercover, go in as someone new to that lifestyle."

"Uh huh. This sounds to me like local and not Federal, so why are we being called in on this?"

"One of the victims is the nephew of a Federal Official, he sits on the Board of Appropriations and the FBI needs his support. As Tip O'Neal once said, 'All politics is local.'"

• • •

Chris's head slowly wagged. "It should be hot and dry down there. I've been covered by the press so I would be recognized. I can't hide my identity and I would need a story that is believable. Let me think on it and I'll get back to you."

• • •

By cellphone, Chris made contact with Lucy Ballard. "Lucy, when I saw you last, you were cute as hell, were sixteen, but you could have passed for fourteen."

"Somehow, I always knew I'd be hearing from you. I'm 5 foot 2 inches tall now, 18 years old, look about 16, I'm still cute as hell, have a fuller butt and bust, I waitress, am making only small tips since this area is now experiencing an economic slowdown—more like shutdown. I live with my parents and save every penny for tuition. In my sleep I still relive Inez bleeding out in my arms."

"Yeah. My sleep is like that. Lucy, we've been tied together by the press. We can't escape that and we could even use it. Would you consider going undercover on a case with me?" He heard her catch her breath. "If you're willing to consider this, then I'll check it out with the boss and get back to you. Meanwhile, I cannot stress too strongly, you say nothing about this to anyone."

Voice catching, she said, "Off the top of my head, I know you will protect. Would it cover my tuition?"

"It would pay well. Definitely, it will cover your tuition. If we do this then I'll be picking up the bills and you will be able to save every dime."

• • •

Chris called. "Lucy, my boss has given me the go ahead so I'll be in Seattle on Tuesday and make arrangements to meet with you and your parents in Cle Elum."

Landing at Sea Tac Airport, Chris rented a car. The drive on Interstate 90, up and over the rugged Cascade Range was through a drizzling rain. His thoughts were on the meeting to come. He asked himself, *Will she go for it?*

Having come down off the Snoqualmie Pass and onto the flat, he drove out from under the rain clouds and clear blue skies appeared. Remembering that long-ago walk he had taken through here as a teenager he thought, *so much has happened since then.*

He exited highway 90 and drove down into Cle Elum. He thought, *this is definitely small town America and hasn't changed much since the time I walked through here.*

Driving East on the main street, he located the motel, booked a room for the night and by cellphone, contacted Lucy Ballard. She drove up alongside his parked car, rolled down her window, and said, "How's the hand?"

He held it up and flexing it, he said, "I exercise the hell out of the first two finger and the thumb; have turned them into a vise. The little finger, I use it to feel along the wall in the dark but that's about all the use it gets."

She nodded and said, "Not pretty but functional. Follow me."

• • •

Lucy's parents, Eric and Edna Ballard, were waiting in front of the house when Chris drove up. Hands were shaken and Eric Ballard said, "You saved our daughter's life." With folded arms, he asked, "So what brings you here now?"

"I want your daughter for undercover. If Lucy agrees to this, we're going to be together and in an intimate relationship with each other. There's risk, but I protect and the pay is good."

Eric nodded, "You do protect! He raised his hands and asked, "What's this about?" How much can you tell us?"

Chris said, "There have been three unsolved murders within the Arizona bondage/discipline community. Our job will be to solve those murders. When I leave you can ask each other all the questions you want. But I have to caution you, you cannot repeat any of what you hear, what you know. So, do you want me to continue?"

They looked at each other, nodded in agreement. Lucy raised her hand to ask a question, then shook her head indicating she had changed her mind.

"Lucy and I have been in the news and that's our cover, our saying that with what we've been through together it has somehow got each of us curious about the bondage and discipline lifestyle, that we want to stick our toes in the water of that lifestyle, and see if this will work for us."

Lucy raised her hand, swallowed, said, "What would I have to do?"

"You would be required to be one of the many, not alone, who in front of others in those clubhouses, would strip, be tied up, be disciplined, and then held and comforted until you recovered. Whether you enjoy it, don't enjoy it, or are neutral, you won't have to fake it, and I don't think you could."

"What about you?"

"For me, up to the point where you would be genuinely distressed, I suspect my providing you with discipline and domination would feel kind of sexy."

Lucy's father was red-faced and bug-eyed. Lucy's mother's mouth dropped open, first in shock, then composed, and she muttered a quiet, "Oh."

"This," Lucy said, "is definitely not the career choice I envisioned for myself when I enrolled at Seattle Community College."

"Lucy, if you're willing to do this, then we will be taking a tour of Bondage/Discipline Clubs from here to Arizona. We're both novices in this lifestyle, and that would be obvious to all. That would be our cover while we work the case."

• • •

Chris returned the next day. Eric Ballard said, "The three of us didn't get much sleep last night. We spent hours on the internet looking into Bondage/Discipline & Sado/Masochism sites. We hadn't even known these sites existed. Okay… yesterday I sat and listened. Today I have questions." Chris took a seat and sank almost to the floor in their spring-sprung ancient couch.

"Would entering that lifestyle psychologically damage my daughter? Would my daughter ever get free of it?"

"You're asking a question I can't answer. You and your wife are big people, your daughter is a shrimp, but what she has, more than anything, is heart. When Chuckie Gross came after her, cornered, she didn't panic, didn't freeze, didn't get hysterical, but skittered about looking for a way out. When I distracted Chuckie she escaped, but she didn't go far before returning to see what's going on, to comfort that dying girl in her last moments. Underneath, this girl is solid as a rock, but more than that, on the surface, she is the most likeable, outgoing young lady I ever met; that's why I want her. I suspect she's got too much heart to remain a waitress. After this case, if she wants it, I can guarantee her a position within the Federal Government."

Edna Ballard looked to her husband. Eric, wife and daughter retreated to the kitchen. When they returned Eric said, "The idea of you whipping on my daughter's bare ass doesn't sit well with me and my wife, plus it's salacious as all hell, but Lucy's choice is her choice."

They both looked to their daughter. She said, "My parents and I want to know, what if I go along with this, and then decide this is not for me?"

"Then you will publicly say that you gave this lifestyle your best shot, you tried it and this does not work for you and you're going home. Meanwhile, I'll have established myself in that community and I will keep on working the case."

CHAPTER SEVEN—Breaking the Case

"Lucy, you will post an ad on the Internet with your picture and the caption, 'R U My Daddy?' To my surprise, that will be where I discover we each share in a common interest. You will take the ad off after three days and that's when I'll return driving a Marquis Motor Home and towing a Jeep. Seattle has a BD/SM Club that's considered one of the country's finest. So we'll stay in Seattle for a week and take in all their workshops."

"Why?"

"Cover. It's a closed society, but within that community the word travels. We need an out-of-state history before we hit Arizona. So along the way we'll also hit clubs in Sacramento and Las Vegas. Then we'll head up to take a look at the Grand Canyon. That will give us the deep cover we need when we hit Phoenix."

• • •

When not at a Bondage/Discipline gathering Lucy didn't wear the slave collar Chris gave her, but she wore it proudly when attending BD/SM events in Seattle, Sacramento and Las Vegas.

Then, also as part of their cover, they headed for the Grand Canyon and spent four days viewing the Canyon.

On arrival in Phoenix Chris phoned Detective Woody Aldridge. "Aldridge here."

"This is Agent Chris Cordel. I'm in Lot 14 in the RV Park on 17 North of downtown Phoenix."

"I know the place. I'll be there in half an hour."

• • •

Woody Aldridge was 5' 9" tall, pudgy, crew-cut, had a large round head, had put in enough time for retirement, but he was not yet ready for retirement—not yet and especially with this case still being open.

Detective Aldridge looked Lucy over and said, "You're with the FBI?"

She gave him a brilliant smile, nodded, and said, "I'm playing his slave, and before you ask, I'm eighteen."

He looked to Chris, who said, "She's my cover—part of the deal."

Aldridge sighed, "Here's the thing. We've been watching this kink world for years, but from the outside. It's private, well-organized, has a clubs here and in Tucson. We have no record of an incident taking place within any of those clubs, or with any of its known membership out in the larger community… until now. We would like to clean up our own messes, we have eyes on the outside watching, but we have no eyes on the inside watching."

Ritch said, "Uh huh. What is it you're not telling us?"

"It looks like something that's happening *within* that community but it feels more like these murders are attacks *on* that community; it just doesn't feel right to me. Plus, the crime scenes are just too damn clean. Whoever's doing this knows what he's doing so even if we knew who committed the crimes, we might not find enough physical evidence to convict. With present day investigation techniques, there's always physical evidence, except in these three cases, there isn't much. Cops are looking sideways at other cops.

Chris nodded, "As paying guests, we've been in other clubs in Washington, California, and Nevada. Most of the others attending were paid up members and knew each other. No guns, alcohol or drugs are allowed and that makes the clubs less risky than your local neighborhood bar."

"Interesting. Hopefully, someone, somewhere, within that movement, has seen or heard something. We need someone inside there who will hear or see what that something could be."

• • •

The Phoenix Club's President went by the name of Angel. She was in her forties, overweight, and gracious. Chris and Lucy signed up and paid the Membership fees. At their first meeting, with members siting in a circle of chairs, Angel said, "We have two new members. I've already met them so let's all introduce ourselves, beginning to my left and going around the circle."

When it came Chris's turn, he said: "Hi. I'm Chris Cordel." He held up his left hand. "Lucy and I met when Lucy was being stalked by a man with a sword. I intervened, got my hand chewed up, and that led to my retirement. That encounter changed each of us in some way and each of us, separately, became curious about BD/SM. Looking on the Internet, I was surprised to see the picture of Lucy, someone I had met under dire circumstances. I read the posting of her R U My Daddy listing, and she's the one I wanted and we're checking it out, looking to see if we want this lifestyle."

That brought an appreciative nodding of heads from the group.

"So here we are. Lucy, you're on."

"Hi. I'm Lucy Ballard. Despite how I look, I'm eighteen. I've always been curious, did some digging for info on this lifestyle, posted on the internet, and Low and Behold, Chris, who had previously saved my life, came knocking on my door. So far, I'm all atwitter. So far I love being his slave!"

What others loved about Lucy was that she was friendly, gregarious, asked lifestyle questions—she sparkled, she listened, and she remembered.

• • •

The first time Chris bound Lucy up and played with her at the Phoenix Clubhouse, and then while cradling her in his arms while she recovered, Ralph walked up and said. "Chris," he said, "Before the arrival of the internal combustion machine, mule skinners, using ten foot-long bullwhips, with only the tip of the bullwhip, would remind a mule to stop dogging it, to step things up. You're using a 2 foot whip. Hang up a balloon and practice, letting the tip of your whip just touch the balloon, that way you will revive an ancient skill, and Lucy will reap the benefits."

"Thanks Ralph. I have a lot to learn."

"Always happy to help."

• • •

Two weeks later, they took a sightseeing trip to Tombstone, now a tourist attraction, and spent the day there. Then they traveled to Tucson to explore it's BDSM scene. Chris' newly acquired expertise and Lucy's exuberance and sparkle invited conversation. Lucy heard it when Diana Finch said, "My ex-boyfriend disapproved of my interest in Bondage/Discipline. He's so moral, so damn smug and superior. That's what drove me away. He warned me that I would be safe only if I turned to him, that women who get involved with these people have a high mortality rate, and his being a Crime Scene Investigator, he knew about these things."

Lucy's eyes and manner revealed nothing, but she had that creepy feeling. The following Wednesday, at a workshop on floggers and their use, she arranged to meet up with Diana. They giggled and Lucy reported, "I lived in Cle Elum with my parents. The Crouse brothers, two of Cle Elum's finest young men, were imploring me to have mercy, to hurry up and choose one of them so the other brother would then be free to move on with his life, to look elsewhere. They were really very decent and attractive young men… and then the older Chris Cordel, the ancient one, came along and swept me away."

"You were lucky," Diana Finch said. "My ex-boyfriend was also older than me, older than Chris, was jealous if I even looked in the direction of another man. After I broke up with him he got even weirder. He shaved off all his hair and even all his body hair."

Hearing Lucy's report, Chris said, "Lucy, call Detective Woody Aldridge."

• • •

Chris and Woody Aldridge paid a visit to the home of Larry Greer. They walked around to the back of the house. "I have the Search Warrant, but if we don't find anything I don't want this man knowing we came looking. He's very thorough. He's working a crime scene now and we have time, but if we leave even one clue he'll know we've been here." Coming to the back door, Woody broke out his lock-picks, said, "My father was a locksmith and I learned from him how to pick locks." He unlocked the back door, said, "You stay out here, don't move, don't touch anything."

An hour passed. Woody came walking around the house from the front, said, "Greer had a toothpick stuck in the crack above the back door. It dropped out when I opened the door. I put it back and came out the front. When Greer gets here I'll walk through the house to the back door, open it, the toothpick will fall out, I'll look out the back door, stare out, then close the door and do a thorough search."

"Woody, as you can see, I'm wearing my hearing aid. I'm half deaf in that ear. Some sounds I can't hear. The W sound I can rarely hear, but with the hearing aid, I can hear some sounds you can't, can hear a mouse walking across the floor. When I walked across that patio on those stepping stones, the sound of the click of my heels on that one stepping stone was different. There could be a hollow place, a hiding place, under that stone."

"Let's take a look."

There was.

They put the stepping stone back in place and waited. When Greer returned home he was served with a search warrant. He wore a calm but indignant expression while Woody made a thorough search of the house. When they went into the back yard Greer was still calm, relaxed, and annoyed. Woody walked around the perimeter of the back yard, checked everything, and began tapping on stepping stones. When he tapped on the fourth stone, he peered back at Greer, kneeled and began lifting the stone, Larry tried to run and Chris took him down and Woody cuffed him. What was concealed in a waterproof plastic bag was a revolver chambered for the 22 long cartridge.

• • •

Woody entered the Interrogation Room. Greer was cuffed to the table.

When the Captain entered the viewing room, and seeing Lucy there, he said, "What's she doing here?"

"She's the one," Chris said, "broke the case." The Captain's eyebrows lifted and then he nodded.

They saw that Greer had a calm look about him, and that felt eerie. He said, "You really don't get it do you?"

"Get what?" Woody said.

"By law, I'm the guilty party, but in truth, I'm the good guy. I was there to protect Dianna. Those were guys who would have despoiled her. I am the martyr and I was out to save her from sin, to preserve her immortal soul."

In the Observation Room, Lucy turned to look at Chris, and said, "Wh-a-a-t?"

"Paranoia," Chris said, "If we accept his premise that those guys were out to rob those women of their immortal souls then everything he's done would be logical and make sense. Always, paranoia will have at it's base, one illogical delusion, that it was them, not him, who was out to rob those women of their immortal souls."

• • •

Chris was never clear in his own mind as to whether Larry Greer was legally sane, whether Larry could tell the difference between right and wrong, or was he faking it? Mental Health professionals and the Courts of law were equally perplexed.

This argument continued to rage even after Larry Greer received a life sentence and was placed in solitary confinement.

Larry Greer had been in Solitary confinement for six months when he hung himself. The argument over whether he was legally insane or faking it was never resolved.

CHAPTER EIGHT—The Caribbean

FBI Director Harry Holbrook paid Chris a visit. "This heat," he said, "takes my breath away. Chris, you were a warrior on the battlefield. I'm a warrior on the political field and I'm fighting to protect the FBI from political machinations. Things will be getting ugly and they'll be trying to come through you in order to get to me."

"Why?"

"It is their intention to install a new FBI Director. Senator Roundtree is out to cast doubt on the overall competence and the character of Individual Agents. It will be Roundtree's contention that it is about time for a little housecleaning within the FBI. He will be questioning the competence of the chain of command within the FBI. They'll be zeroing in on you as their initial target, as an Agent who has outlived his usefulness as an Agent, as an agent who can't cut it anymore and is being kept on the payroll for sentimental or political reasons."

"Uh huh. So they'll be coming after me in order to get to you."

"You got it."

"This pisses me off. I don't need this."

• • •

Chris was called before a Senate Committee. Senator Roundtree was chairing the meeting, tapped on his microphone for silence and said, "Let us begin. I call on FBI Agent Chris Cordel."

Chris came forward. When he was seated behind the mike Chairman Roundtree said, "What I have learned Sir, is that you have a crippled left hand, need a hearing aid, that you have nightmares, that your education ended in the Ninth Grade and that you engage in sado/masochistic practices. How did a man like you ever manage to be certified as an Agent of the FBI? You are physically handicapped and yet are employed in hazardous cases, plus, I only recently learned you are sexually abhorrent Sir."

"I believe," Chris said, "the word you're searching for Senator, is aberrant. As to whether I am aberrant, or as you say, abhorrent, that is not for you to say. It would be useful Senator, if you were to consult a dictionary before you start bandying about words you don't understand. This is nonsense."

Roundtree, sounding ominous, said, "Sir, you are very close to being in contempt."

"Not close… I'm already there. This is beyond ignorance." His voice dropped a pitch. Rising, he said, "This disgusts me and I'm leaving!"

Chris arose and headed for the door while Senator Roundtree pounded his gavel and bellowed, "Take that man into custody!"

An Officer in plainclothes stepped in front of Chris and said, "Secret Service. I'm sorry Sir."

"No problem." He held out his wrists, was cuffed, and was patted down. He shook his head and said, "Left my gun at home."

• • •

Chris was brought before the Judge, who said, "What's the charge?"

The Prosecuting Attorney said, "Contempt of Court Your Honor."

The Judge looked up. "How so?"

"The Defendant is an FBI Agent who disagreed with the Senator's line of questioning, and attempted to walk out of the Hearing."

"If disagreeing with one of our Senator's is a crime then we are all liable. How does the Defendant plead?"

"Guilty as charged," Chris said.

The Judge stared. "The Defendant, who appears to be of sound mind, pleads guilty." Shaking his head, the Judge said, "Does the Prosecution have anything to add to this?"

"Your Honor, the Senator has refused to withdraw charges, the Defendant, FBI Agent Cordel, refuses to withdraw his Guilty Plea, and we must acquiesce to the Judgement of this Court."

"Dropping it on me are you? I have a headache coming on. Bail is set at $10,000." The gavel came down.

Chris said, "Your Honor, I will not post Bail."

The Judge stared, put his hand to his forehead and in a reluctant voice said, "Bailiff, take this man into custody."

The Judge's head had begun to throb.

• • •

Roundtree was privately chuckling while publicly saying, "This is a sad business. If Agent Cordel continues in his refusal to cooperate with our Investigation, he will be convicted of Obstruction. The FBI has placed this unqualified man in harm's way many times and their motive for doing so has yet to be determined."

Shockwaves spread. The following morning, Chris Cordel was still refusing to post Bail, refused the services of an attorney and the News Media was having a field day reporting on the case. Senator Roundtree offered to withdraw his charge of contempt if Chris was willing to testify.

Chris declined the offer.

Reporter Joanne Muir said, "Senator Roundtree, are you saying you are willing to destroy the career of a decorated war hero, of an off-duty and unarmed FBI Agent who took on and subdued a sword-wielding lunatic who had already butchered three and was not yet done?"

• • •

When asked, Director Holbrook stated, "I will say only this, the rumors we were hearing have panned out but the why of Senator Roundtree's assault on Agent Chris Cordel still remains a mystery."

A reporter asked, "Why do you think he is doing this?"

"You'll need to ask the Senator that question. What I can tell you is that Agent Cordel, on the morning following his arrest, sent me a letter stating he was unwilling to testify in a Kangaroo Court, didn't wish to disgrace the FBI, and therefore he was offering his resignation from the FBI."

"Did you accept his Resignation?"

"I did not! Any of us may be vulnerable to unsubstantiated character attacks, but Roundtree will find it difficult to attack Cordel on his record since, both as a military man and as an FBI Agent, his record is exemplary."

• • •

Senator Roundtree blustered, but by day four it became clear that public opinion had turned and that Senator Roundtree had misjudged, had made a mistake. Chris was unceremoniously kicked out of jail.

On being kicked out of jail, cameras were blinking and someone said, "Officer Cordel, what are you going to do now?"

"Director Holbrook has ordered me to take a vacation. I haven't had a day off in years so maybe I'll do that."

"If your letter of resignation had been accepted, what would you have done?"

"I thought about that. I have no head for business but I'm pretty good at picking up on what people are up to… I don't know; probably go back to bartending or work as a bouncer. Now you'll have to excuse me, I'm tired. Being an honest cop, I wasn't exactly popular with my fellow inmates and things sometimes got dicey. I've collected a few bruises, have sore knuckles and will now have a substantial bite scar up close to my right elbow."

The scarring, they saw, would be substantial. Chris had secretly rubbed in cigarette ash so as to enhance the scarring. The camera zeroed in, did a closeup on a swollen and raw bite wound.

"You'll have to excuse me; I want to catch up on a little shuteye."

They had their story, the waves parted, and they let him pass.

• • •

Agent Chris Cordel showed up at the office of Director Harry Holbrook at 5 PM. He said "It gets dark early this time of year."

"It does, and the political climate has grown wintery and very dark for Senator Roundtree. I knew Roundtree would be coming after you to get to me, but what I didn't know was what kind of counter attack you would mount. How'd you know to do that?"

"I was hearing reports that vague questions were being solicited to confirm that I was no longer able to perform my duties… others were being asked what it was like working with me; did they feel safe working with me."

"As to your question, there was this Confederate General… I can't remember his name… I read that when his troops were being harassed from the front and the rear he ordered, 'Split the Troops and attack in both directions.' I took that as my cue and did the same.'"

Nodding, Holbrook said, "Your counterattack put Roundtree on the defensive. Politically, he's still blustering, but having you jailed, having you confined in a space where you would have ample opportunity to demonstrate your ability to handle yourself in a physical confrontation, he's drowning; he's now dead in the water, the wind is now out of his sails and I suspect he will never get back underway."

• • •

Chris and Lucy flew to New York—they had lunch with Dawn Tyler. Chris said, "How's it going with you and the Strauss Corporation?"

"Not good. I've about had enough. I told Abel Strauss that either his son goes or I go and I damn well meant it."

Dawn had informed Strauss Inc. that she would not be available for the rest of the day. It was a beautiful Fall day with clear skies and a brisk breeze, and Chris, Lucy, and Dawn went for a walk around the reservoir in Central Park. The three of them had dinner together. When Lucy took a trip to the ladies room, Dawn said, "Chris, I know that you and Lucy will be parting company, each of you heading in a different direction, but I want to hear more."

"Lucy and I, along with her parents Eric and Edna, will be taking a vacation at Cannon Beach on the Oregon cost. We'll be on the beach when my Service records, along with the unreleased details of my hand repair job will find their way into the media. This is overkill and I am not happy with it. Lucy and I, along with Lucy's parents, will be vacationing on the Oregon coast when my Service Record, material not released before, will miraculously become public.

Learning of this I will give expression of my chagrin at this invasion of my privacy. Of course Director Holbrook will be annoyed by the unauthorized release of this material and steps will be undertaken to see that this does not happen again.

$$\bullet \ \bullet \ \bullet$$

There were two clothing stores in the town of Cannon Beach. Chris succeeded in getting Lucy's father to try on a pair of short pants, an aloha shirt, and beach shoes. He paid for Eric's purchases while Lucy had a similar success with her mother.

The four of them had a fabulous seafood lunch and then, the tide being out, they went for a walk on that glorious beach.

The sun was hot, the sky was a cloudless pale blue, and they were being caressed by the cool breeze coming in off the water. Eric, with Edna standing by, said, "Chris, taking a vacation with Lucy and her parents, this makes you look like Mr. Wholesome. Other than political shenanigans, you have any other reason for doing all this?"

"You're Lucy's parents, and I enjoy watching the three of you together. You are a neat family. Lucy has informed me that while our time together has been a grand adventure it's not what she wants for the rest of her life and she will be returning with the two you to Cle Elum and then she will disappear into Writing Classes at the University of Washington. I'm enjoying the short time we have left together and I'll miss this wonderful girl, but then it's over."

"Why? Eric asked.

"According to her, Lucy's experienced enough real-life drama that writing drama fiction is now all the excitement she really wants. She says small-town life now has it's appeal."

"Sounds to me like you're dumping my daughter."

Chris shook his head. "Other away around. She's dumping me. Then, I will disappear into the Caribbean and keep my head down until the dust settles. Lucy's tuition for next year at the U Dub has been paid for. After that, Lucy and I could possibly get back together. I'd like that and we've talked about it, but I don't think it's going to happen. The bondage/discipline was different—interesting for awhile but it's over."

CHAPTER NINE—Meet Trish Nelson

Chris Cordel was ferried from Miami to the Bimini Islands. Looking about, the rental house he found was spacious, had lots of windows, and was situated on a narrow tongue of land between the harbor and looked out on the open sea. The house was shaded by palms and from the porch, he could walk down the bluff and across the white sand to the ocean. In the green light of the water over white sand, he could see the shadow of any big fish long before they could come close to the beach.

The views were a feast for the eyes.

Chris was assured it was safe to swim near the shore during the day, but he was also told that at night sharks came in close to hunt. Each day Chris ran on the beach. Running in the soft sand gave him the serious workouts he wanted. Running barefoot also sandpapered his feet and so he returned to wearing sneakers. Then, after that, he would cool off by going for a swim.

Late afternoons he would break from these solitary pursuits to wander down on the bay side to shop, walk out on the docks where the cabin cruisers were tied up, have supper before dark, and maybe have a drink.

He grew more relaxed and more at peace each day.

Bernie Hamilton was the bartender, was amiable and kept the conversations centered on the here and now. "Bernie," Chris said,

"I suspect you never asked a direct question in your whole life. Why not?"

"There are things I probably don't want to know."

"Like what?"

"Like why you're here? Like why are those four cabin cruisers tied up to this dock? Two of them are occupied by retired couples but I don't want to know why the other two are here and I don't want to know."

• • •

The richest of the Cabin Cruisers was occupied by a powerfully built large man—a gentleman named Bruce Bartell.

Chris was at the bar and passing time with Bernie Hamilton's attractive wife when Bartell, who seemed to think he was irresistible, walked up and said, "Honey, I've got millions, so why don't you drop this loser and come away with me."

She threw her drink at him while Chris rose smoothly from his chair and faced Bartlett, who feignted with a left and then threw a right. Chris easily slipped the punch and doubled Bartlett over with a left hook to the liver. Chris said, "If you want to continue this, why don't we do it outside?

Recovering, Bartell said, "Sounds good to me." When Chris turned towards the door, Bartlett threw a punch Chris again avoided.

Chris did not want this over quickly—he took the time to break Bartell's nose, bent it over to the left side, and then bend it over to the other side.

"Even in Paradise," he said, "you run into assholes. You Dumb shit; I'm FBI and you're a fucking mess! Now get out of here and stop bleeding on the floor! You go out and come back with a gun and I'll have an excuse to shoot your sorry ass!"

• • •

For some time, Chris had traveled either with the two-barreled Derringer in 32 cartridge, or with his Sig Sauer automatic.

He made some phone calls and found out that Bruce Bartell is heir to a huge fortune, his family is very big in the research and the distribution of pharmaceuticals, and Bartell had skipped out on a

$10,000 Bail for busting up some guy in a Miami Strip Club. Chris thought, *nice guy our Bruce.*

Chris was on the dock and Juan Carrillo was on the deck of his cabin cruiser when Chris said, "Morning." Juan was a lean middle-aged man with a full short beard. Looking up from what he was doing, he said. "Morning, rumor says you're FBI."

"Not at the moment. Politics got in my way and I'm currently on a leave of absence. When and if the political waters calm, I may go back."

"Why you telling me this?"

"So you'll know. Not many people here I can talk to."

"I have a son in a wheelchair and going to college, I have responsibilities."

"Juan, I'm not after you. Have a good day."

Chris walked off the dock while Juan stared. Once he saw that Chris was headed for his rental unit, Juan sauntered up to the bar. Bernie Hamilton was behind the bar and recognized the twitch in Juan's eye; Juan was troubled and ordered a beer.

Bernie brought the beer, set it down, and said, "Juan, I usually don't involve myself. But I saw that man fight. If I were you I wouldn't run, I wouldn't fight, cause… if he want's you, he will definitely get you."

• • •

Days later, when Chris entered the bar, Bernie said, "Looks like two heavy hitters just entered Juan's boat."

"I didn't know you would involve yourself."

"There are times when I don't always have a choice."

Chris had the two-shot Derringer in 32 caliber in his right front pocket. The wind was up and Chris entered the choppy water from the far side of the dock. He worked his way up to where he was forward of Juan's cabin cruiser, dove under the dock and came up on the far side of Juan's boat. He raised himself slowly onto Juan's deck. On entering the cabin, the one with the gun swung about but too late, and Chris shot him in the forehead. The one beating on Juan went for his gun but was dead before he could lift it. Chris untied Juan and said, "Friends of yours?"

"Not any more."

"Tell me about it."

"I transported drugs for them. If I'd been caught, I never would have said a damn word, but now with this, if you see to it that my son gets treated right, I will sing like a canary."

• • •

Bernie Hamilton was put in charge of Juan's boat while Juan was being escorted to the States.

The helicopter was noisy. DEA Agent Trish Nelson escorted Juan Carrillo and Chris to Miami. Agent Nelson was an olive-skinned and blond beauty, had terrific looking strong legs, and her bust, bottom, and lips were lush and fulsome.

Chris didn't care for Miami vacationers, thinks the beaches are too crowded, strip clubs turn him off and he will enter them only when it's part of the job. Also, he doesn't appreciate being jostled by people that are loaded. But especially, he thinks those desperately trying to have a good time in those clubs need to go elsewhere and get a life.

What he did appreciate on that trip was the view when Trish went forward to speak with the pilot. Her bending forward gave him a spectacular view of her butt. Chris was definitely a butt-man.

Did Trish know she was being appraised? For a brief moment, she appeared to pause.

Chris thought, *the women in my life, Dawn was tall and elegant, Nancy was taunt and pretty, Lucy was tiny and vivacious.* What a remarkable specimen Trish truly is.

Juan Carrillo had said, "Before I say anything. I need a guarantee that you will see that my son is able to complete his education and will have a job waiting for him when he graduates."

Trish Nelson said, "Granted."

• • •

"Trish," Chris said, "why were you chosen for this assignment?"

"No male Agent was available at the moment. They reported your military and FBI history, your history with Lucy Ballard who submitted to being tied up and having you whipping on her ass. What about Nancy Poletti? Did you tie her up and whip on her ass too?"

"I did not."

"Also," Trish Nelson continued, there is a rumor that at present you are living alone and looking to recruit another woman into your sick lifestyle."

"Nelson, I don't need this shit so get the hell out of my face!"

• • •

A day later, Trish approached Chris and said, "I think I owe you an apology."

"Why? Is it because you were told to apologize or is it because you owe me an apology?"

"I definitely do not want to believe I owe you an apology, but what I think is that maybe I do owe you an apology. But who are you? What are you?"

"What do you see when you look at me?"

"A tough guy, a survivor."

"Uh huh. I will ask you this, if you had not heard the rumors, seen the scarring, Seen the hearing aid, would there be all this tension or would we be comfortable with each other, go to dinner together, walk around the park, talk about the books we like, what they have taught us, the movies we like, things like that?"

"Chris Cordel, You're scar-faced, have a crippled left hand, a bite scar on your right arm, a hearing aid and you are dangerous. But if I weren't already engaged, I would probably be attracted to you, and since I'm engaged I'm saying to myself, this man could break up my relationship."

CHAPTER TEN—Anna gets her degree

FBI Director Harry Holbrook called Chris Cordel to his office. "Chris," he said, "two weeks ago I was in a store line while the two ahead of me were openly talking about the two deaf guys ahead of them. I realized then that others will talk openly in front of a deaf guy if they think he can't hear them."

"Why you telling me this?"

"Because I know you're studying sign language and I'm wondering how I can use this. To change the subject, there is a man and woman bank robbery crew out there hitting small rural banks, this team has hit five banks in the last eight years."

Chris said, "Any constants?"

"We think the woman cases the bank first, reports to the man who then comes in, robs the bank, then she is driving the getaway car when he comes out of the bank. Sometimes one of the serial numbered bills will show up at one of the minor casinos… never at one of the big casinos."

"So they're keeping their heads down."

"They are. I have an uneasy suspicion, based on nothing concrete, that some of their expertise, may be leaking from the Banking Community."

"You're telling me this and swearing me to secrecy because?"

"Because each time we get a handle on their current MO, they pull a switch. And I don't know where they're getting their information. I've even interviewed some of our jailed bank robbers, looking for a heads up. One of the jailed robbers, said: 'they're good, but also, they're working with inside info."

FBI Director Harry Holbrook put in a call to DEA Director Bernard McSweeny "He said, "McSweeny, you've made good use of my Agent Cordel. I could use the services of one of your Agents from time to time. Under special circumstances, I think we could help each other."

• • •

Trish Nelson was driven from Sea Tac Airport to Seattle's Olympic Hotel. She picked up the key reserved for her.

She unlocked 4B, entered, saw Chris, the bellhop set down her suitcase, closed the distance between them, and without a word the two of them embraced. "Dammit Chris, there was a spark lit when we were in Miami, and now it's ignited. I'm embarrassed."

"What about your relationship?"

"Not anybody's fault, it just fell apart."

Chris nodded, said in sign language, "How's your signing?"

She signed, "I've been working on it."

• • •

"Chris" Director Holbrook said, "our two robbers are damn careful. The driver is a white woman, the man is white and about 5 foot 9 inches tall and about 160 pounds. We know they play low-limit poker. Twice, serial numbered bills from different robberies have shown up at the casino in Wapato Washington. I suspect they may live in the area and that's why banks in that area has never been hit. It's a long shot, but possibly they may return to the Wapato Casino."

Walter Pearlman had formerly been a bank teller, lived in the area, and his uncle, Milt Pearlman, was a retired FBI Agent who had worked bank robbery cases. Chris and Trish could have waited and watched, but deciding to push the envelope—they brought in long retired professional gambler Frank Grady—who annihilated the Pearlman's low-level poker game. Then strapped for cash, the Pearlman's attempted another bank job, and when Walter Pearlman came out of the bank the FBI was in waiting while Edna Pearlman was already in custody.

• • •

"When I was still with Dawn," Chris said, "I realized my hearing was not getting any better, and I asked her if there was a different sound when someone calls her by the name Dawn and when someone calls a guy Don? She said that sometimes she could hear the w sound, sometimes not.

Chris shook his head. "I can't hear the difference. I'm not sure… I may have heard the w sound once upon a time, but for sure I can't hear it anymore… not even with hearing aids, not since Afghanistan."

• • •

"Agent Cordel," Director Holbrook said, "Meet Detective John Casey."

They shook hands and Casey said, "I'm working the murder of one of our civilian employees. Chris, how proficient are you in sign language?"

"Medium. I'm better at reading than I am at signing."

"The victim," Casey said, "Patty Steinberg, was friends with Louis Johnson. Louis is gay, teaches at the school for the deaf while his boyfriend, Wesley Hardin, is deaf. We have a witness who reported having seen Wesley pitch a bitch in sign language when he discovered Patty and Louis having coffee together. Louis was signing back angrily, no words were spoken, but our witness says, the imploring looks Louis cast at Patty, plus the angry looks Wesley cast at her, made it clear that the argument was about Patty Steinberg."

"What role am I to play in this scenario?"

"We're having a certified signer in to interpret when I interview Wesley. After the interview Louis and Wesley will be placed in a waiting room with another who is waiting and that other will be you. You will ask Wesley a question, will get pissed when he doesn't answer, Louis will tell you that the guy is deaf, you will look confused, and hopefully one of them, in sign language, will let something slip that has relevance."

"Uh huh. That could maybe work."

• • •

Prosecutor Spence said, "I now call FBI Agent Chris Cordel to the Stand." Chris was sworn in. "Agent Cordel, how do you know Louis Johnson and Wesley Hardin?"

"They were placed in a waiting room with me."

"Why?"

"I read sign language. It was suspected that Wesley Hardin or Louis Johnson, in sign language, might reveal issues that were pertinent to this case."

"And did they?"

"Mister Johnson, in signing, asked Mister Hardin if he had been the one killed Patty Steinberg? Mister Hardin said in signing that he couldn't have since the tracks leading up to where Patty was shot were made by a size eleven sneaker, and that he wore a size nine."

"And why is that pertinent?"

"There were tracks in the mud leading up to the murder scene, those tracks were made by a size eleven sneaker, and this information had been withheld. The only way Wesley Hardin could have known about the sneaker tracks and their size was that he was the one wearing them."

"In your opinion did Mister Johnson have any culpability, any inkling of what was going to happen to Miss Steinberg?"

"No culpability. Only a suspicion after-the-fact. I see Mister Johnson as a man shaken by the death of a friend."

• • •

Wesley Hardin pled guilty and received a ten to life sentence. Louis Johnson said, "Agent Cordel, I thank you for my friend, and I thank you for not judging me."

Chris's head flew back. "Johnson, I'm sorry you got outed. You're an intelligent and decent man and I'm sorry you lost your friend and your job at the school."

"Thank you. I'm going to miss teaching but I'll survive."

• • •

When Chris returned to New York, Chris and Dawn, both for practice and to keep their discussions private, in public, often communicated using sign language while giving facial expression to their emotions. Others, seeing this and assuming they were deaf, would openly express thoughts and feelings they would have otherwise kept private. It was amazing what people will say when they believe others can't hear. It became a game they played, and once, they actually heard the plans for a liquor store robbery. The robbers were apprehended as they came out of the store and the robbers never found out how the cops knew and were waiting for them. Dawn, prompted by Chris, had taken up signing as a hobby, but the chief difficulty in all of this is that Dawn's not a cop, can't fight, and can't shoot. She admitted, "I arose to the occasion that one time as best I could but this is not what I want or who I am."

• • •

On the day Anna Stern marched up to the podium and received her BA Degree in Social Work, she saw Chris Cordel sitting with her beaming brother Charley. Grinning from the stage, Anna held up her diploma for them to see, and blew a kiss to each of them.

After the ceremony Chris waited while Anna exchanged hugs and kisses with her former classmates, accepted a hug and a peck on the cheek from her brother and then watched his retreat. Soberly, she approached Chris and leaned her face into his shoulder.

"After that first year," she said, "I couldn't do the hooking anymore, so I took the job at Starbucks. But that first year, I had to keep hooking or I would have crashed and burned. When I stopped hooking, I felt lost—like I didn't know who I was anymore."

He nodded, "Same thing with my scarred face. Plastic surgery could remove the shrapnel scars, the one on my lip, my hair could be allowed to grow long, but if I did that I'd be lost. I wouldn't have known who I was anymore—I'd be so good-looking, so wholesome, I'd want to kill myself. Why go through that when I don't mind the scars, they tell people I'm a soldier and reminds them not to mess with me. It's going to be a clear night and I'd like to take you to dinner and we could view the city looking down from the space needle."

It was a beautiful star-filled night, and Anna was glowing. The Space Needle Restaurant was perched on a tall stand rising up high in the air, was reached by elevator, and the restaurant turned slowly on its axis and they looked down on Seattle and across the Puget Sound to the Olympic Peninsula. "Chris," she said, "you're white, have money, are FBI, you're athletic, you work out, you run, your left hand is bad scarred and your face is scarred but that only makes you more mysterious, so why are you zeroed in on me when you could get whoever you want?"

"Anna, you're a damn good-looking black woman with a terrific smile, face, and figure. Still, I had to ask myself, *why do I want you rather than Claudett Neeson?* She's taller than you, white, has a great education, has family, position, has a sexy body same as you and is one of the most classically beautiful woman I have ever seen, is elegant, her family is rich, politically well-connected and she could probably marry the President, even *be* the President if she chose. In short, she's a winner, so why is it that I want you when that most remarkable woman has made it clear that she would welcome my attention?"

Anna's eyes narrowed. "Tell me why."

"At that time I couldn't have told you why because I didn't know. Physically, intellectually, and sexually, Claudett and I were a good match but emotionally we were a disconnect."

"Why?"

Emotionally, she sees herself, rightly, as a winner. Objectively, I've won in every battle I've ever fought but there was always collateral damage and that makes me a survivor rather than a winner. Emotionally I'm more like you. We're both survivors, and that provides me with an emotional connection to you; plus I've always wanted to jump your bones."

"Uh huh! So why haven't you?"

"That would have turned me into a trick and I wanted more than that for each of us."

Anna said, "Goddamn," leaned over and kissed him.

• • •

"Anna, Seattle Community College and the square world is located within walking distance of the mean streets you grew up on and so you wouldn't have felt totally lost, but now it's time for you to move up and on. The University of Washington is located smack-dab in the center of middle-class Seattle. I can get you into a two-year Social Work Program at the UW."

Anna stared at the floor, raised her eyes, said nothing.

"You're not big but you're good looking, strong, athletic, have innate intelligence, are a severe undifferentiated character disorder. While a character disorder is not good, emotionally, you're as steady as a rock, have a lousy background but good genes. When you graduate in two years, if you're still single and I'm still single, then we might choose to marry… even have a child."

Again, Anna muttered, "Goddamn."

CHAPTER ELEVEN—Criminal Pride

Anna said to her brother, "Let me digress. Digress is one of the big words I've picked up. In the beginning, when Chris Cordel offered me two hundred not to accept my two years Scholarship, I hated him more than you can imagine. I looked like an Angel, a sexy one, but as you know, I was one angry chick.

"I took pride in being able to walk into an alley, bend over, lift my skirt, and pick up a quick hundred, so who was he to think that I would bend over, trade in my scholarship for two hundred."

Charley had agreed with her that Chris Cordel had been disrespectful, and had said, "We need to show that honky bastard how dumb he is."

It had taken Anna to the middle of February to wise up to the fact that Chris had conned her, had hooked her into being angry with him, and that her brother Charley had been in on the con. Also, her Guidance Counselor Dora Davis, who was blacker than black, had also been in on it.

Anna had let them know how angry she was and they all agreed that she had every right to be angry with them. They all agreed that it was a miracle that she had stuck with it and not gone back to the mean streets she had known. Her criminal pride at being a slick know-it-all chick was taking a serious beating and she found it hard to stay angry when they all agreed that she have every right to be angry. Damn! Anna's anger, along with her criminal pride, was losing it's potency; so how impotent can you get? Anna stroked her anger the best she could, but her criminal pride went limp, was refusing to stand up.

Brother Charley commiserated with her. "Yeah. That criminal pride. Thinking back I can see where I made all kinds of mistakes but still I got away with it and that allowed me to keep telling myself that I was slick, was some kind of master criminal. It felt so damn good being this master criminal that I had to brag about it and that brag got me doing hard time."

Anna nodded. "It's changing for me too. Anymore I don't take pride in having been a streetwise, know-it-all hooker.

• • •

Guidance Counselor Dora Davis set Anna up to conduct a series of jailhouse interviews as part of her fieldwork.

Jake Renard was a good-looking con. He was tall, confident, handsome, even charming. Intent on impressing Anna, he turned on his nice smile and beautiful blue eyes and modestly reported, "Every time I went to jail I learned something."

Anna's eyes went big and she said, "I'm impressed. In the past fourteen years you've been arrested only four times, beat the charges once, most of the charges were pretty mickey mouse so you've only served seven years total. Not a big price to pay for all you've learned. And, in the next fourteen years you can probably expect, since you're a lot smarter now, only another two or three arrests. But with your jacket already showing three convictions you'll be getting longer sentences and that's not so bad because you'll have the time to pick the brains of other smart locked-up guys.

"That will allow you to continue telling yourself how smart you are while you are living more than half your life in a cage with others not half as smart, as knowing, as you. When you get locked up again, rather than getting down on yourself, keep on reminding yourself how much smarter you're getting."

Jake did not look happy, not so confident, as he was being led back to his cell.

• • •

Anna learned of the case of Kerry Patterson's wife who had been murdered. Along with the police investigation, Patterson also hired a private detective to look into the murder of his wife. This additional effort to find the murderer of his wife would of course alleviate any suspicion that Patterson had anything to do with her murder, his being so anxious to avenge his wife.

The only problem was that the private detective discovered the identity of the one who actually committed the murder and the murderer provided evidence implicating Patterson as the one who had commissioned him to kill Patterson's wife.

Learning of this case, Anna shook her head while saying to herself, *criminal pride, that self-aggrandizement of the self as a slick master criminal, has struck again.*

Even street hookers, as had Anna, take pride in being street-wise hookers. Having now jettisoned her own criminal pride at being a streetwise hooker, Anna sometimes felt confused, light-headed, but even so it kept her safe while her former defiant criminal pride had kept her teetering on the sharp edge of the cliff.

• • •

Guidance Counselor Dora Davis said, "Anna, as a Social Worker, probably your first job will be in the addiction field. A constant in the addiction field is Alcoholics Anonymous. You will need to know AA from the inside out, so we're giving you a stay at a three-day marathon AA Conference, plus expenses, plus the motel registration, in Seaside Oregon."

Anna took the bus to Seaside and when she arrived more than 200 attendees were milling about and totally accepting of each other. Some were in quality business suits while others were in sneakers and T shirts, but none of that seemed to matter. Hard to believe—but they all acted as if they were the best of friends while Anna felt totally alone.

Maddie Olson and her husband Ollie Olson, an older couple, were in the Motel unit next to Anna. Maddie said, "You appear to be alone and don't know anybody so perhaps you will join with us for dinner?" More in shock than she would admit, Anna accepted their offer. They put her at ease and sort of adopted her.

Ollie was a big 72 year old retired fisherman. He spoke with a Norwegian accent, and he and Maddie had been married for 48 years while Ollie had not taken a drink in the last 44 years.

After dinner, they went to the hall for the first Meeting, took seats in the front row with Anna in the middle between Ollie and Maddie. Every time the first speaker said something, the crowd would break up in appreciative laughter. Anna didn't get it. She thought, *are these people retarded?* She didn't see the humor.

The second speaker told the story of how he came out of an alcoholic blackout knowing only that he was somewhere in the Alaskan wilderness and had no idea which way town was, that it was over 20 degrees below zero, that he didn't have matches, and if he didn't get back to town soon he was going to freeze to death.

He said: "I raised my hands up to the sky, and said, "God, it's in your hands now. Send me an Angel to show me the way back to town." Then the speaker's voice arose. "God," he said, "wasn't listening to me, I saw no Angel! And I would have froze to death if some Eskimo hadn't come along and showed me the way back to town!"

The room cracked up, and this time Anna got it. A singing sound was going off in her head and she thought about her own Eskimos, thought about her brother Charley, her Guidance Counselor Dora Davis, but most of all, she thought about Chris Cordel. She thought, *I'll be damned. There is a God watching over me, and Chris Cordel is his angel.*

Ollie was one of the night's speakers and Anna was mesmerized. Ollie spoke with a definite accent, said tink for think, dot for that, but it wasn't long before Anna didn't hear the accent, only what he said. What did he say? Anna didn't remember, the words went right through her, but the emotion, a feeling of comfort, of acceptance, went into her.

• • •

"Ollie," Anna said, "I don't get it. You're all so accepting of each other, accepting of me. I see guys in expensive suits and guys that carry out the trash sitting down together and being totally accepting of each other, like you all belong together."

"Anna," Ollie said, "what we all share is a common bond, a

desire to stop drinking. You haven't got there yet. You drink too much, you think you should stop drinking, but what you want is to keep on drinking."

Too true. How did he know?

That that night, when Anna took the Jim Beam out of her suitcase, she stared at it and didn't take a drink that night.

• • •

After the Conference, Ollie drove Maddie and Anna back to Seattle. Sitting in the back seat, Anna said, "Maddie, you have children?"

"We had a daughter. She was in the military and died in Iraq. You remind me of her sometimes. You have parents?

"My father was killed when a drug deal went bad. My mom was white, was smart and educated but a loser who hooked up with my dad. I was 13 when my mother died of a drug overdose. My 15 year-old brother and I took to the streets. He burgled and dealt drugs while I hooked. We never thought of going legit and we've both done stretches, me in Juvie while my brother did hard time."

"Uh huh, and now you're in the UW's Social Work Program. Maddie said, "Ollie and I have talked. You work at Starbucks and we live just across the freeway from the University District, our daughter's bedroom is empty, and the University is within walking distance. The only thing we ask is that you don't bring alcohol or drugs into our home. If you do, you're out."

Later, Anna would ask herself, *is Chris Cordel behind this? Wouldn't surprise me.*

• • •

Anna moved in with Ollie and Maddie and also attended open meetings with Ollie. Open meetings were meetings open to those not in AA. She liked the people she met there and said, "I wish I could belong here, but I don't think I'm an alcoholic."

Ollie shot that down saying, "The only requirement for membership in AA is a desire to stop drinking. That's all it takes."

Ollie then took Anna to a closed meeting. For the first time Anna stood up and said, "My name is Anna, I'm an alcoholic, and

I have four days."

Applause and shouts of 'Welcome' greeted her. It felt so damn good. After the meeting, she said, "Ollie, will you be my sponsor?" He shook his head. "Anna, that wouldn't work. A man, especially an old man, sponsoring a girl, especially a young pretty girl, that wouldn't work. Plus, when I look at you, sometimes I'm not seeing you, I'm seeing my daughter. But I got someone I want you to meet."

Maisy Berneau was bigger than life, was white, had a huge ass, walked with a cane, had been sober almost as long as Ollie, and could see right through people.

• • •

Chris showed up four times during the two years Anna was at the University. Anna turned out for the Woman's Track Team, and on her second year, she made the team. At the UW Track Meet, Anna looked up and saw Chris sitting in the stands with her brother Charlie, Ollie, and Maddie Olsen. Anna scored a third in the broad jump, was a decent middle-distance runner, and was on the winning relay team. On each of his visits Chris had dropped money on Maddie before he left saying, "I'm not going to be here so you use your own judgement as to when and if to give her money."

Learning of this Anna said, "Why does he keep doing this?"

Maddie said, "I don't know. Couldn't be because he sees you as a pretty girl all alone in a hostile world after losing your parents. Probably you're just some social experiment he's conducting to see which way you're going to jump."

"Moments like this," Anna said, "God how I hate him."

Maddie didn't hide her smile. Anna hugged herself. In her own mind, Maddie and Ollie had become Mom and Pop and she loved them dearly.

• • •

Anna's brother Charley went to see Dora Davis, Anna's former Guidance Counselor. Charley said, "Miss Davis, you helped my sister finish a two-year program here. Now she's in her second year at the U Dub, and that's a lot tougher. If I go to jail it might mess up her program so I don't want to chance it. I need all the help I can get to stay out of Jail."

"You have charges on you so you want me to intercede on your behalf?"

"No charges, and no charges pending, but I'm still slipping and sliding. I need to get out of this life. As my sister says, 'Criminal pride, puffing yourself up for being such a slick-assed criminal, it feels good at the moment and that's why we keep feeding the fire, it feels good, but it's a damn killer, sets you up and lands you in the slammer."

Dora's initial look of disbelief melted into curiosity. "Give me a number where I can leave a message and I'll get back to you." Three days later, Charley received the call. "Okay." Dora said, "I made some calls. Evidently, no one is looking at you for anything. You can use me as a reference and I'll tell what I know."

Three months later Charley visited Dora Davis. He said, "I want to thank you. I'd been working at the Stendahl Corporation for nine weeks, and for the first two weeks I thought the job was going to kill me, plus, there were so many opportunities to steal, and I called myself a pussy for not stealing when I had the chance. Can I take you out for coffee?"

"God I hope you're not conning me. And yes, you can take me out for coffee. Charley, tell me about criminal pride."

"More than anything, it's what gets us locked up. When I was 18, I pulled off a big score. There was a guy I didn't trust but still my criminal pride kicked in and I couldn't help myself, I heard me bragging to this guy I didn't trust about how smart I was, about my big score. That brag got me doing hard time. After I got out, I took pride in having decided to be a little guy, to never again do any job worth bragging about. Then I took pride in being too slick to do a big job. Now, working for Stendhal Corporation, a job you got me, I saw the ways where they were vulnerable, how and where they could get ripped off. For the first time it disgusted me to see my criminal pride rising up. That prompted me to go to the Senior Stendhal and explain to him how and why they were vulnerable to being ripped off."

Dora said, "Was that criminal pride?"

"I don't think so. For the first time in my life, that thinking disgusted me, told me I was thinking like a dumb-assed criminal.

Stendhal stared at me, thanked me, and when I got up to leave, to get back to work, he came from behind his desk and walked me to the door. Three days later, when we closed down that day, when I was walking out the door, a guy was waiting by the door and said, 'Charley Stern,' and my heart sank.

"The upshot is that now I'm working for Burns Detective."

"One thing," Dora said, "always puzzled me. You and Anna are well spoken except when you lapse into street talk."

"Or is it the other way around. Our Momma was white and educated. My sister and I play with language. We either sound educated or we talks street talk."

• • •

All my life, Anna thought, *I've had the face of an Angel and a heart as cold as ice. Now I seem to have thawed out and even share some of my thoughts and feelings with my square sisters in the Program.*

"Maisy, You're my Sponser, and my life has been such a waste. Chris Cordel has done everything for me and I've done nothing for him."

"God how dramatic." Maisy said, "Anna, get your sorry ass off that self-righteous pity pot! You've been given the chance to reach out to others who still suffer. God's given you the chance to serve others so be grateful for that!"

• • •

Charley Stern and Dora Davis married, and the two of them would have three children. The Stern's were close to Chris and Anna, and one day Charley would move up to management after a long career as an undercover agent for Burns Security.

On his most famous case, Charley was relocated to New York City and went to work as laborer at the Queens Copper Refinery. Copper ingots were disappearing and since each ingot weighed over 300 pounds, they were not going out in someone's lunch bucket.

Two days later Charley called Mister Trimble, the head of the Personnel Department and said, "As a laborer, I can't move around. Transfer me to the Watching Department where I can move around, see what's happening." Trimble made the transfer.

Jack Kelly, another watchman, took time to check out Charley. "Your accent, I can't spot it."

"West coast, Seattle."

"Why you here?"

"No reason, just wanted a change of scenery.

Kelly nodded, "Uh huh. From time to time, I've also felt the need for a change of scenery."

Charley nodded.

• • •

After working his shift, Charley was walking up to catch the elevated back to Manhattan when he passed Kelly who lived nearby and was installing heavy-duty springs in the rear end of his pickup.

A week later Kelly said, "In the time I've been working here, I've figured out probably a dozen ways I could probably steal copper ingots."

Charley gave a brief shake of his head and said, "Three things. First, those ingots weigh 315 pounds so you can't do it alone. Second, you'd need to be damn careful about who you bring in on it. Third, don't do it on my watch."

Jack Kelly worked on charley and was eventually able to recruit Charley into joining the crew stealing the copper ingots.

The day came when Charley called Head of Personnel Trimble and said, "When you go home tonight, don't have anything to drink, and wait for the call."

At 9:05 Trimble received the call. Charley had broken the case. Kelly was quick to testify against the others including Henley, who was the head of the Watching Department and a former Manhattan Lieutenant of Detectives who had been forced to retire as a Policeman with a pension of $75 a month. The Judicial system was angry and this time around Henley was going to do some serious time.

CHAPTER TWELVE—Isler's Story

Harvey Isler had been with the FBI for five years when Chris Cordel met up with the guy wielding the samurai sword. At that time Isler had been the Junior Partner working the Bierman case. Bierman had been to his Safety Deposit Box, left the bank, entered the parking garage and was shot down. The FBI found nothing. No one heard or saw anything. All they had was the ejected cartridge case and the bullet that had rattled around in Bierman's skull.

Agent Isler, along with lead FBI Agent Petterson, had checked out every possible lead and found nothing. The case went cold and Agent Petterson retired. That was then.

Now, Harvey Isler was called to the Office of Director Holbrook, who was looking grim, and said, "You're to reopen the Bierman case. We received a tip, the rumor floating around Walla Walla Prison is that it was an FBI Agent who robbed and killed Bierman. I have accounted for the time of every Agent we had in the area at that time; except I can't account for Chris Cordel. He was in the area and enrolled at Seattle Community College at the time. We didn't even know he was in the area until that guy with the Samurai sword came after him. I don't believe a word of the rumor, but we still have to check it out. But remember, this man is Chris Cordel so if it comes to that, don't even think of taking him down without serious backup."

Harvey took Agents Bell and Scott with him. He didn't try to bullshit Cordel, saying, "You remember the Bierman case from when you were at Seattle Community College?"

"I don't remember the Bierman Case. What's going on?"

"You were enrolled at Seattle Community College when Bierman was shot. The rumor is that it was an FBI Agent who killed and robbed Bierman. You carry a Sig Sauer. We need to check your weapon."

The way Chris looked at them… it was tense. He said, "Damn! You assholes are too lazy to go and check out that rumor. If I go get my weapon it'll give your sorry asses an excuse to start shooting so either I'd kill you or you'd kill me… someone would die. My gun, it's in the closet. Go get it and then get the fuck out of my house!" Chris was much pissed.

The next day, Cordel called, left a message saying he's taking a leave of absence, and booked a flight to Los Angeles. Director Holbrook said, "It could be a miss-direction. He's done that in the past."

The gun they had taken from Chris Cordel had not fired the bullet that killed Bierman.

From Los Angeles, Chris had rented a car and drove to Las Vegas.

Harvey decided to investigate the how and the why of the rumor that an FBI Agent had been the shooter. The up-side of this investigation was that one of those Harvey interviewed at Walla Walla Prison, feeling smug, had said, "I knew you guys would be coming to me. I want some consideration for what I can give you."

Agent Harvey Isler said, "You have something we can use then definitely you will get consideration.'

"I know who did it. It wasn't an FBI guy who shot Bierman."

• • •

It was clear that the interviewee knew details of the crime not released to the media. Now having a line and pursuing this line, Harvey Isler was able to identify the shooter, and knowing where to look, they gathered enough evidence to make the arrest and eventually, when the case finally does get to Court, they will convict. Agent Harvey Isler called retired Agent Petterson and said, "We can now close the Bierman case. We know who did it."

• • •

Harvey traveled to Las Vegas and located Chris Cordel who was then working as a bouncer in a strip club. When Harvey talked to the club manager, he said, "This guy's just under six feet. That's not very big for a bouncer."

The manager nodded, said, "Even bigger guys, when they size up Chris, see something in the eye of this scarred up guy, and the way he carries himself, that usually warns them not to get stupid, not to tangle with this guy."

Cordel was not smiling when Harvey approached, but he was curious. Eyes alert and narrowed, he said, "Why you here?"

"I came, Harvey said, "to return your gun, but also you were right and we took a look at how that rumor got started. Finally, we know who killed Bierman and can close the case. Petterson was my lead on that case and it bothered him to retire with that case still open. I called him last night, let him know we can now close the case.

"Chris, controversy swirls around you like a thick fog but Director Holbrook wants you back on the job and says I'll be transferred to Alaska if I don't get you back."

Cordel slowly wagged his head from side to side, his face broke into a hint of what could have been a grin. He said, "It's hard to stay angry with someone who will spread that much horseshit just to flatter me. I need to cool off. Call me tomorrow. I'll be thinking on it."

By phone, Harvey reported to Director Holbrook, who said, "You saw the hint of a smile on his face?"

"I did. You think he was conning me?"

"Nah. It'll take him 24 hours to cool down but then he'll be back."

• • •

Chris and Harvey Isler were in Seattle and in the elevator at the King County Courthouse with a sleazy looking guy who had a mouthful of rotting teeth. Chris pushed the button and stopped the car between floors and, turning to Rotting Teeth, he said, "You're holding. Slowly, show some ID." Rotting Teeth showed his badge. Chris said, "Uh huh. Narcotics?" Rotting Teeth grinned and nodded.

• • •

No one was neutral on the subject of Chris Cordel. Some saw him as a hero while others viewed him with suspicion. Chris was to learn that back in DC, a Kangaroo Court of Supervisors had convened and marched on Director Holbrook. Spokesperson Bell said, "Agent Chris Cordel breaks every training procedure, does not always measure up to our dress code, sometimes is seen in a leather jacket rather than in a dark business suit, has a crippled left hand, has a hearing aid, has taken two unauthorized leaves of absence, disappears, and when he returns from out of the blue, you welcome him back with open arms. If I, or any other Supervisor, or any of the Agents we supervise pulled this, plus the fact that he is half deaf, I think you'd fire us."

"Yes I would."

"So how come Cordel gets away with this?"

"Because he's Chris Cordel. You're good all of you, but if any of you ever get in a tight spot, you'd be damn lucky to have Chris Cordel at your side."

Harvey Isler, hearing this, tended to agree.

CHAPTER THIRTEEN—Meet Mad Dog

Chris flew from Seattle to Washington DC. "Chris." Holbrook said, "we have a problem. The fact that I have continued to assign you to active cases even though you have a damaged hand, a hearing aid, my providing you with other exceptions to the rule, has provided Senator Crabtree with an opportunity to engage in some malicious speculations. He would like to oust me as FBI Director and replace me with his choice for the Directorship. How's the strength in that hand?"

"Holbrook, every night for years, I have rigorously exercised my left hand and I have no doubt that the fingers I have left, plus my thumb, now compared to the digits of my right hand, are much the stronger. No question, my left thumb can damn-near punch holes in the back of another man's hand. My left thumb and first two fingers are vise-like and no longer suited for delicate work. The little finger I use mostly as a guide touching the wall as I walk in the dark."

• • •

Senator Crabtree, along with Agent Rose and Supervisor Hajer entered Holbrook's Conference Room. They took seats. Holbrook, Isler and Cordel were already there and seated. Crabtree said, "We all know each other so I'll get right to the point. No one questions the bravery or the willingness of Agent Cordel. What is in question is Agent Cordel's physical competence and fitness to respond to the eminent hazards one runs into in the field. It has come to my attention, Director Holbrook, that you assign physically handicapped Cordel as the Lead or the Backup in dangerous assignments. This endangers not only Cordel, who we all know is a brave man, but it also endangers other Agents!"

Holbrook turned to Chris and said, "How's the strength in your left hand coming along?"

"It gets a little stronger all the time."

Crabtree bellowed, "Gets a little stronger! That's not good enough!"

Mildly, Chris said, "Any of you left-handed?"

Agent Rose raised his left hand. Chris slowly extended his left hand, Rose accepted the challenge and clasped the hand. Chris buried his thumb into the back of Rose's hand while his three fingers flexed and moved on the hand he held. The slight concave shape of the palm of Rose's hand was being reversed. Still kneading and compressing what was within, Chris turned his head and said, "Crabtree, I'm always ready."

Chris was still punishing the hand he held. "Will you concede that I am physically able to perform my duties?"

"I'm not ready to concede that."

Rose screeched, "Fuck! He's wrecking my hand!"

Chris released the hand. "Hajer," Chris said, "Somehow, I think you had something to do with this."

Director Holbrook stirred, said, "Crabtree, you've been suckered. Hajer, you went over my head with this, you jumped the chain of command. This infraction has earned you a demotion, you are no longer a Supervisor, and you might think about purchasing some snowshoes."

After their departure, Holbrook said, "How'd they ever get the idea your hand was incapacitated?"

"Along with my other workouts, I give the vise-grip of my left thumb and the first two fingers a workout to their limit every night I'm home. Only thing I can come up with is I'd just finished my hand workout when Agent Rothschild showed up, saw my hand fumbling while I was picking up my hat. Rothschild may have said something and Hajer could have picked up on it.

"All these years of doing this workout has not been boring since I always suspected that this day might come along. I've reached the limit of how strong the hand can get and I'll stay at this level as long as I can. What're you going to do about Agent Rose?"

"He'll be left here to spread the word about what happened. Then, when he's grown comfortable, we'll let him join his buddy Hajer up in Alaska. Chris, you've disagreed with me, even defied me, but you never went behind my back. More than I can say for those two assholes. The DEA has requested your services for another assignment in Arizona."

• • •

By phone, DEA Agent Turnbull said, "Cordel, you remember Corporal Hector Hernandez from your time in Afghanistan?"

"Hector? Yeah, I remember him. Skinny guy who could put away more beer than any man I ever saw. He always had some kind of a scam going, found cute ways to get his hand in your pocket, but in the field he was a soldier, a true warrior. You could trust him with your life but not with your money. So, what about Hector?"

"We have his younger brother, Juan Hernandez, in custody. Juan has a vivid imagination and you need you to work on that. Hector read about you taking down the guy swinging a samurai sword. He read about you being likened to a mad dog that just keeps on coming. Hector took up the name Mad Dog while retelling his little brother the Afghanistan stories. He always referred to you as Mad Dog. Juan knows some things we'd like to know, so we'll have you work on his imagination; we'll let him know that you were brought there specifically to conduct his interrogation."

• • •

The next day, Chris flew to Tucson, took a chair outside Juan's cell and sat. He watched Juan. After three hours, Juan came to the bars and said, "I see your left hand. You the one they call Mad Dog?"

"Some have called me that."

• • •

Officer Turnbull brought Juan his lunch tray. Then, curious and deferential, he said to Chris, "Sir, why you staring at him?"

"Getting to know him saves time."

Officer Turnbull, an hour later, brought Chris a cup of coffee and a stack of reports. He began studying the papers. Two hours later Turnbull returned and still differential he said, "Sir, the weather report predicts Dust Storms across Highway 85 tomorrow."

Chris, not looking up, nodded. "Uh huh. So, if you were transporting a prisoner you could get blown off the road, the prisoner might even escape into the desert and he might never be heard from him again." Turnbull nodded solemnly, "And we would assume he made it to Mexico and didn't come back! I get it. Case closed."

The next day Prisoner Juan Hernandez was told, "Get ready to be transported to San Diego."

Juan said, "By way of Highway 85?"

"Yeah . . .. How'd you figure that?"

"Tell them I'm ready to talk and right now."

• • •

Chris flew back to DC.

CHAPTER FOURTEEN—Anna to the Rescue

Chris was in Seattle's Northgate Mall walkway when automatic gunfire erupted and there were sounds of people running and screaming. Chris was moving towards the entrance to Sears as people were pouring out into the walkway. The last thing Chris remembered was the blaze of everything turning white.

• • •

Chris awoke, He couldn't see. He tried to reach for his face and realized he was in restraints and couldn't reach his face. A choking voice said, "Don't try to speak. You can't. Your face and jaw have been shot all to hell while the shock has knocked your eyes cross-eyed and taken out all your teeth. Amazingly, your tongue is swollen but was spared from permanent injury. The whites of your eyes now have a nice purple hue but we think they will recover in time. You're breathing through a tube inserted in your throat and your eyes and vision will recover in time. Meanwhile, lift your right hand signifying we can take you into surgery and start making repairs."

He raised his hand.

• • •

Director Holbrook was informed. "Get me the hand signer Louis Johnson, also get Anna Stern and have them at the hospital when I'm flown in."

Holbrook arrived, and along with Johnson and Anna Stern, they were briefed by Supervisor Harris. They learned that Cordell's jaw, nose, and cheekbones were shattered in multiple shards, some quite small, and hand signing was the only way Chris could communicate. It was clear that the shock alone should have been enough to kill him and he was right up to the edge.

Holbrook asked, "Does he realize how damaged he is?"

Harris said, "I think he does, and knowing how bad it is he may not care whether he lives or dies. At best, he has numerous surgeries ahead of him. He has to keep on fighting or he'll die. I'm bringing in plastic surgeon Doctor Sharkey to do the repairs. If there's anyone can put that face back together it's Sharkey.

Hearing this, tears were running down Anna's face.

Director Holbrook now assumed command. "Anna, I know everything there is to know about you including the pimp you dumped and the drugs and alcohol you kicked. Anna, this is where you come in. Sympathy, as you know, won't work with this man. We don't need your tears right now. Being tough is something you do well so do it; get pissed… get after this man for leaving you. Tell him off. Get him pissed off enough and he just might decide to go on living."

Anna's eyes stopped leaking tears, "First time I've cried," she said, "since my Momma died. Okay," she turned to Harris and said, "When do I see him?"

"They'll mask you like the medical staff, and you've got time while they start prepping him. This is the bad one where they repair the roof of his mouth. Go get him tiger."

Anna walked in, said, "Jesus Chris, you've been shot all to hell! They told me you've run out of fight… really pissed me off." She shouted, "I told them they're full of shit! You never going to be as pretty as you was, but damn it Chris, you took me off the streets, got me into the Community College, then into the U Dub. You took me away from the only life I knew so you owe me to shepherd me into your world, to care for me, and father my children." Tears dried up as she shouted *"Damnit Chris, don't you dare die on me!"*

Chris turned his palm up, waggled his fingers and Anna put her small hand in his.

Years later Chris spoke of how not alone he felt having her

cool hand in his. Then the anesthetic kicked in and the nurse said to Anna, "You can walk with him while we take him into surgery.

• • •

Louis Johnson and Anna were in the Recovery Room when Chris came to and began signing. Louis pushed the button. When surgeon Tom Starkey, a big fat fellow, arrived, Louis said, "He's signing, asking how the surgery went?"

"Chris, it took me four hours, but I was able to re-assemble the roof of your mouth. The support medical team was damn good, kept you alive, kept you from crashing while I worked. That was the toughest surgery and now we can start rebuilding you a face. You have other surgeries ahead of you, and by the time we've rebuilt your face and provided teeth implants, you're going to be damn sick of doctors, but the upside is you'll have a long life and teeth implants that will last forever. The downside is you are never going to be pretty."

Chris signed and Louis interpreted. "He's asking what happened to the shooter?" Anna jumped. "You didn't know? The two bullets in his chest came from your gun. You got him."

He signed. "I don't remember."

Titanium implants were utilized to put together the salvaged bones of Chris's cheeks, nose and jaw. Coming out of surgery, still mentally loopy, when Anna held his right hand to her cheek, he ran his hand up into Anna's hair, then down her face, across her breast, his hand fell, and he was out cold for another twenty minutes. No one said anything; they looked at Anna. She said, "He never did that before. I don't think he's going to remember this, and if he doesn't, I don't know if I'm ever going to tell him."

After two more surgeries, the breathing tube was removed, Chris's face was functional enough that a semblance of garbled speech was returning, but he was far away from being articulate. Then, after having the teeth implanted, at least four more surgeries were forecast.

"Chris," Anna said, "I've known you for five years and not once have I had sex with you. I clocked your pecker rising from time to time, but you never jumped my bones. I knew you wanted me, and I knew you were sleeping with other girls, even knew who the girls were sometimes, but never with me. I always wanted to show you how good I was. But you never jumped my bones. How come?"

He signed, "I wasn't willing to risk you classifying me as a trick."

"You were right, and you not treating me like a hooker put some serious hurt on my hooker's pride, so eventually, it took more than two years, I took pride in not being treated like a hooker. You are a devious bastard Chris Cordel."

• • •

Chris went into crisis mode, there was a rattle and his breathing became labored. "Anna," Doctor Sharkey said, "I'm a surgeon and this new development is out of my league. We're bringing in Doctor Dubois. He's the best Diagnostician I know."

Anna was a constant, held vigil in a chair placed so she could see the door where hospital staff wearing hospital scrubs were moving in and out. When they wheeled out Chris on the rolling cot she jumped up and said, "what's going on?"

One of the RN's said, "we're taking him for cat scans and then we'll bring him back."

The doors to the Restricted Area closed in front of her and Anna returned to her chair. A female RN, without speaking, brought Anna a cup of coffee and a toasted cheese sandwich. Anna nodded her thanks and tears rolled out. She thought, *everyone is being so goddamn nice.*

After Chris was wheeled back to his room Anna watched as Doctor Dubois moved in and out reading reports and looking at charts and then, after huddling with surgeon Sharkey, he approached Anna.

"I'm Doctor Dubois. Your boyfriend has what looks like asthma but is not asthma. He has pneumonia. Whether he picked up the bug before he came to the hospital or after, the pneumonia has had time to advance. Still, despite his labored breathing and erratic heartbeat, his oxygen level and blood count is good and we've shot him full of antibiotics. Tell me about him."

"He's a tough mean man. Piss him off and even tanks better get out of his way."

"So others tell me. Now, as a diagnostician, I need to tell you that you look like hell. Right now, you're on the edge of collapse and you need to get some rest."

Anna was led to a small room down the hall and stretched out on a cot.

• • •

Doctor Sharkey said, "Anna, we'll be watching for the unlikely prospect of him having an allergic reaction to the antibiotics but he looks good to go for the repairs on the nose and cheekbones that will make the face at least functional. Then we can start on repairing how he looks but no way he will ever be pretty. He knows now that he has pneumonia but this surgery will be a walk in the park compared to those other surgeries, risky in his present condition, but we've decided to go ahead with it."

The purple of the whites of his eyes had mellowed down to pink and were no longer crossed. In the past his eyesight had been about as good as human eyesight gets, but even so, it was suspected that in the future he would need reading glasses.

"Anna," Louis Johnson said, "he hand signed me that he's not going anywhere, that you sound like a shadow of yourself and you need to get some rest."

"Him being this damaged and he's thinking of me, God how I hate him for being so fucking nice."

Nurse Johannson said, "I have to ask, would you be comfortable napping on a cot in the same room with Mister Johnson?"

"Absolutely. We're brother and sister in this."

Anna and Louis Johnson were led to a small room with two cots.

• • •

Two more surgeries and Chris signed, "How long has Anna been here?"

"Fourteen days."

He signed, *All I can put together is four days. I must have been really out of it.*

Hearing Louis's report of this, Anna said, "That you were Big Ugly; that you were."

Speech was garbled, not decipherable, not yet, but Chris could sign. "Anna, if you are willing to be seen on the arm of this Big Ugly, and you being the one who rings my chimes, if I get through this,

I'd like to marry you."

She kissed the back of his hand—that he could feel.

He signed, "I love those lips."

• • •

Emergency Room Supervisor Doctor Andrew Lippicott sent word to Louis Johnson that he would like to speak with him. When Louis showed up, Lippicott said, "Mister Johnson, everyone in our Department speaks well of you. Also, when they brought in that injured Norwegian and he could not understand our questions you stepped in and interpreted. So, in addition to sign language and Norwegian, do you speak other languages?"

"A little German."

"Remarkable. You're a certified CPA, you've spent time here on all shifts so you are familiar with what we do here. You live nearby?"

"I live across the street from the South side of Woodland Park Zoo. If you're asking me whether I would like to work here the answer is yes.

"I'll notify our employment office that you'll be coming by and that we want you."

CHAPTER FIFTEEN—A Decision not to film

Chris, on being discharged into the care of Anna and RN Beverly Adams, was seen every day by Physio-Therapist Charley Adams. "Chris," he said, "you were a wreck but in only 21 days you've regained four pounds, you're now taking walks around Greenlake, takes you damn near three hours to walk the three miles, you're working out with light dumbells and getting stronger every day. Others might never recover fully, but you have a ton of natural stamina and if you keep on working like this I predict you'll have good strength and decent stamina back in a year. It was a pleasure working with you, but you don't need me anymore, and you can now do this on your own."

"Thanks Charley, I appreciate all you've done."

Chris continued working with his speech therapist.

Director Holbrook showed up. "Chris, I have plans for you and Anna. You and Anna will be married in her church, Pastor Honeywell will perform the ceremony and I'll be picking up the tab.

"Ritch, I checked your bank account. You have more wealth than me and I'm far from poor. Plus, you will be receiving another monthly Government check for the damage to your face in the line of duty. Then you will be driven to the Bridal Suite at the Olympic Hotel and in the morning the two of you will be flown to Miami where you will go aboard a yacht the DEA has seized. For six weeks the two of you will cruise the Caribbean. Anna has yet to find out she will be marrying a wealthy man.

When Chris and Anna married, Maisy Berneau, leaning on her cane, was the Bridesmaid, was probably the oldest bridesmaid in Christendom, and Ollie Olson walked the bride down the aisle and gave her away, Louis Johnson was Chris's Best Man, Maddie Olson, plus Anna's brother Charley were there, and the South End church was packed.

• • •

Director Holbrook had said, "As part of your honeymoon, two of the crew, a male/female team, will have the task of teaching the two of you to dance to jazz, and will be monitoring your progress in that area. Chris, that'll give you the exercise you need, all you can handle at this time. I don't think either of you could have married anyone but each other and you are a romance for the ages—you two belong together—you will cruise the Caribbean, the two of you will learn to dance to jazz, and Anna, when you return, you will have a job at the U Dub waiting for you. Both of you give your brains a rest and get yourselves primed to go to work when you get back."

• • •

After the wedding, by limo, they were driven to the Olympic Hotel where they were already registered in the bridal suit. Chris picked Anna up to carry her into the bridal suite.

"I can't believe it," Anna said, "my feeling so shy."

• • •

Across a table of soft foods, they couldn't seem to lower their eyes from each other. Anna said, "Six years, but we finally made it."

Anna wheeled the table into the hallway, came back, gave Chris her hand, they entered the bedroom and closed the door.

• • •

The next day Anna and Chris were flown to Miami and were met by Agent Harvey Isler who escorted them to a waiting vehicle.

When they boarded the yacht Echo, lines were cast off and Echo headed out to sea. The Echo was not large. After the evening meal, they headed to the open small deck where Vern and Leona provided an impressive demonstration of dancing to jazz records. Vern said, "We've been tasked to teach you jazz dancing. You're never going to be as good as us," *this challenge evoked a stare between Chris and Anna*, "but in six weeks you could be pretty good."

Retiring to their cabin that evening, Chris said, "Were they challenging us?"

"I don't know. It could have been their ego," Anna said, "or it could have been a challenge." She came into his arms. "Enough of this. For years it was an ego thing where I wanted you to want to take me. It's different now, not an ego thing anymore. Big Ugly, for me you are so beautiful and I flat out want you, want your children."

His being strong enough now, he picked her up and carried her to their bed.

• • •

Leona and/or Anna would dance with Chris and would not stop until Chris began to shake, to stagger; then Anna would dance with Vern.

While Chris was recovering Anna and Chris would stretch out on deck chairs and, holding hands, would stare out at the waters and skies.

"Chris, I am amazed. For the first time n my life I just flat out want a man and for some strange reason, you just happen to be that man."

"Even this worn-out scar-faced old white guy? I've wanted you for five years but I wouldn't cop to it. I think I was right."

• • •

Six weeks later, docking in Miami, Chris had recovered seven of the twenty plus pounds he had lost during his hospital stay, was tanned, was stronger but not yet full strength and still far short of his former stamina. He and Anna took a cab to the Airport. When seated in a quiet corner of the departure lounge, Anna said, "Why is our flight delayed?"

Chris shrugged, "It could be a mechanical problem, could be

logistical." He was relaxed, comfortable with now being with his beautiful wife and at the moment it did not bother him that others stole looks at his scarred face. When he was relaxed, not tired, the stares did not bother him. At the moment, it was their curiosity, their problem and not his. Anna could tell however, that when he grew tired, the stares still irritated him.

Then Newscaster John Morton, with microphone in hand and cameraman at his side said, "The chance that an FBI Agent would be present when a man chooses to go on a killing rampage is way less than one in a million. Mister Cordel, you've been Johnny-on-the-spot twice. How did you know?"

"Jesus. Morton, did you come up with this on your own, or did someone put you up to it?"

"Our Station's slogan is 'The Truth Others Dare Not Speak.'"

"Morton, think man. Think about how I might respond to this provocation. You're kind of a dumb ass and I suspect they set you up to be filmed with me kicking your butt. Think about what could have happened with me still mentally loopy and you coming at me like this?"

Morton was silent, and Anna said, "My husband's reputation for ferocity is not exaggerated. He is fierce when it comes to protecting others or himself. So, again we ask you, what kind of a story could possibly come out of you bugging my husband like this?

Eyes big, Morton hesitated and said, "Possibly something lending credence to the thought that your husband, has something to hide, and therefore the FBI, had foreknowledge of the attacks to come?"

"You wish," Anna said, "show this film without blurring out my husband's face and you and your station will be in big trouble."

They decided not to air the film.

CHAPTER SIXTEEN—Dixie Lands Club

Marty Hogan and Rich Rinzler had each received a note with instructions and two crisp new $100 bills. The instructions stated they were to meet in a certain hotel room on a certain day and at a certain time. They did.

The gentleman they met was wearing rimless glasses and a three-piece suit. He said, "Think of me simply as The Banker. This job is big, has been in the planning stage for over two years."

Rinzler raised his hand, "How big?"

"Thirty million big. Fortunately, I determined that two of those previously selected for this undertaking are unreliable. They will be replaced, hopefully, by you two. Yet we still need to determine how resourceful and reliable the two of you are." He handed each of them a packet.

"In each packet you will find detailed reports of time and place for two separate payroll deliveries by armored truck. The driver will be alone as the payrolls are small, only about $30,000 each, not much, but enough to test your resourcefulness and integrity. There are also detailed instructions of where and how you will deposit my 50% share of the proceeds from these endeavors. This is a test. If you fail to carry out this assignment, fail to deliver my share of this endeavor, I lose nothing, and I will be gratified to find out that you do not qualify for a more serious undertaking. From this undertaking I will take only $5,000,000.

"I will stay in this country and my primary satisfaction will come from seeing a job well done while each of you will share equally in the plus $25,000,000, and will be provided with transportation to a country without an extradition policy."

• • •

"Chris," Director Holbrook said, "We have had two armored truck robberies, two weeks apart, one in Seattle and one in Portland, and you are now the Agent in Charge of the Seattle Office."

"You're kicking me up the ladder? You think I can't cut it any-more on the streets?"

"That's part of it. Doctor Dubois tells me that it will take you another two years to regain your formerly formidable stamina. You are probably the only Agent in the history of the Bureau who would look on this promotion as a negative. I know how much you hunger for the adrenaline rush from the hands-on, but you're not yet up to full strength and you have a live wife who needs a live husband. Plus, I have future plans for you and your wife. I pulled your military records."

"Why?"

Holbrook waved away the question. "Despite your lack of formal education, your test scores were all high while your General Aptitude and Clerical Aptitude scores eclipsed your Mathematical and Mechanical Aptitudes by a quarter mile, but because by instinct you are a warrior, instead of clerical training, you opted for training as an Infantry grunt."

"So?"

"So now it's time for you to step up. I need you as a Case Manager. We have two Armored Car robberies on the west coast. I want you to case manage the Seattle robbery while Floyd Costa has the Portland robbery. Two different banking firms and yet each was hit on a day when they were transporting a payroll. That could be a coincidence but we think not. Your wife has a job waiting for her at the University, plus her AA Sponsor lives in Seattle, so there you have it."

On the flight to Seattle, Anna was seated by the window and

staring out while the two of them held hands and grooved on each other. Another passenger, across the aisle and two seats forward, turned and with his cellphone, snapped Chris's picture. Chris arose, confiscated the cellphone without speaking, and returned to his seat. The gentleman sitting directly across from Chris said, "You're Cordel. I was a rookie at the Police Academy at the time when you took down the Sears shooter. That was all we could talk about. You still use a hearing aid, your hand's all chewed up, your face then got all chewed up and yet you nailed the shooter. People stare at you and then look away. How do you deal with that?"

"You still on the job?"

"I am."

"What's your name?"

"Artie Weiss."

"Understand, Officer Weiss, it was the presence of my wife-to-be that got me through the surgeries."

Anna, at this time, still holding Chris's hand, leaned over and stared at Artie. "Officer Weiss," I'm surprised he's opened up to you like this."

Chris turned, "Anna, with you holding my hand, him being candid about staring, he had his part, you had your part, and the third part was enough time has passed that I have now adjusted, it's not as bad being the Big Ugly as I had thought it would be. For good or for bad it damn sure does get me noticed and remembered."

• • •

The house in the Wallingford District was perched on a high lot, two storied, had a wide covered front porch, three bedrooms, a bathroom on each floor, a basement apartment and bathroom, and had a generally comfortable and old-fashioned look. The owner, Frank Betger, was widowed and a retired Seattle street cop. He was alone since his daughter and son-in-law had moved to Berkley California. Frank lived in the basement apartment and the upper floors were for rent. They liked Frank Betger and so Anna and Chris moved in.

Anna was put in charge of the Outreach Program at the University of Washington and supervised both men and women who had been placed there on Parole. It was her responsibility to monitor her

Parolees and to violate them if and when they screwed up and send them back to the joint. She learned that those fresh out of prison, damn near all of them, first thing, would get loaded and then get laid. She didn't advertise it, but first time around, she'd let it pass. Those who didn't get a grip, she would violate and send back to the joint.

Often, those she violated were those lost souls who had grown up in an unstable environments, and even though they all protested how much they hated prison, many made dumb mistakes and secretly welcomed a return to the three hots and a cot, the stability, and the time they had to socialize when let out to the yard. Anna recognized these differences and most nights Anna slept well. There were also those cases where addiction to crime, addiction to drugs and/or alcohol were the culprit and Anna had to violate them. Those cases were not rare.

Still, Anna did have her success stories.

• • •

Chris was the Agent-in-Charge of the FBI Office in Seattle and found that he did not miss the action in the streets as much as he had thought. Supervising provided its own adrenaline rush; it was not as high but it lasted longer and was quietly addictive. He drove to Portland to confer with Agent-in-Charge Floyd Costa and they spent the afternoon comparing notes on the two Armored Car robberies.

During dinner, Floyd said, "Too many similarities. Both robberies were made when the Armored cars were carrying a decent payroll, both times the driver was alone making the delivery, both times by two masked armed robbers who drove away in a stolen car and abandoned it. We found one foreign fingerprint on the back of the rearview mirror, our FBI Data Bank hasn't found a match yet but they're still looking."

• • •

FBI Agent Terry Neal was a decent bowler and poker player—made a little money at both— and promptly spent it on women and cognac. When word came back that they had identified the print found in the getaway car, Agent Terry Neal was still, then asked, "who?"

Chris reported, "Marty Hogan."

Agent Neal, in a relaxed voice said, "Oh. I know who that is. Hogan's a righteous con, could have got a reduced sentence by naming the others, but he rode the beef, you catch him, he's not going to tell you anything."

Chris bobbed his head to avoid showing the stillness he felt. Later, when alone, he pulled Agent Neal's case files, left a message for Anna saying he didn't know when he would be home. Searching, he found nothing in Neal's file to indicate he had ever had contact with Hogan. Then he went the internet to look at Hogan's record. Again, he found nothing indicating any connection with Agent Neal. Alone and out loud, he said, "Neal, you narcissistic bastard, you couldn't resist showing off how much you knew."

At seven Anna called and said, "You okay?"

"I'm okay but I'm not a happy camper. I'm looking at something pretty nasty. I have to get some of the things rattling around in my head sorted out before I'll get in a car and head up Highway Five towards home. I'll either be headed home in an hour or I'll let you know."

• • •

Again, Chris drove to Portland to consult with Floyd Costa. "My wife is the social worker running the program monitoring cons coming out of prison and into her Outreach Program at the U Dub. She came up from the streets and she's one smart tough cooky. She said Hogan sounds like one of the Humpty Dumpty's who, when they get kicked out of prison, fall apart and can't be put back together again, one of those who miss's the stability, the three hots and a cot that prison provides."

Costa looked up. "I remember the poem Humpty Dumpty. Sounds like Marty all right. He lived with his mother down on Burnside and as a kid he went hungry half the time. When things got crazy where he lived, as they often did, he would take off, flop wherever he could. He was popped several times and did small stretches. Then he was the small cog in a big-time robbery, we caught him, and offered him a walk to testify against the others. He refused, took the hit for everyone, served five years. He's basically a nuisance, not usually considered a serious problem, and if we arrest him he's not going to testify against the other guy, so we'll put him under surveillance and see who he relates to."

Agent Terry Neal was on vacation in Las Vegas and was reported to be winning at the tables and spending lavishly.

· · ·

At the close of the Jazz Festival Chris said to the clarinetist, "Big Daddy, as you have seen, my wife and I can dance."

Big Daddy Basque said, "That you can, but without that you'd still draw a crowd."

Chris nodded, "My wife and I can't afford public scrutiny. We can't be known for visiting a particular public place. Is there some place private where we wouldn't be hassled by crowds, where my face wouldn't draw a crowd, where I wouldn't have to arrest someone or shoot someone? Anna and I are looking for a place where we could just dance. If there is such a place we sure would like to know where that place could be."

Big Daddy took out his handkerchief, wiped his sweating brow, looked off in space, looked back at Chris, and said, "How can I reach you?"

· · ·

Big Daddy Basque visited Chris at his office in the Federal Building. Chris arose from his desk, extended his hand, Big Daddy shook it, and sat. Big Daddy said, "There's a private club on the South side, no whites in it. I told them about you and your wife, told them about your problem, your need for privacy. They understood that, but the management, asked how comfortable would you be in an all black club, and how comfortable would they be with having a scary scar-faced old white man in their club."

"I resent that. I'm not old. I just have a lot of wear and tear."

"That you do. They told me to have you and your wife come Friday night. They need to see for themselves. They've never let in a white and if they let you in, let you join, you'll be the last."

"Sounds good."

· · ·

The name on the door said 'Dixie Lands Club.' Chris had no idea where the name came from and didn't ask. When Anna and Chris entered, everyone stared, tried not to let on, but they stared. Club President Dave Everguard introduced himself and said, "Now I understand why we never saw your picture in the paper."

"Give them time, "Chris said, "When the shock wears off they'll stop staring."

"The staring bother you?"

Chris shrugged, "Not so much anymore."

The musicians, following Big Daddy's lead, stopped tootling their instruments and swung into a number. Anna grabbed Chris's hand and dragged him to the dance floor. People stared at them but then switched to watching how they danced. One woman said, "Can't believe it. That scar faced old white man can dance alright."

After the number, Chris led Anna off the floor, and Mary Everguard, tall, in her mid-forties and overweight, said, "Chris, will you dance with me?" He took her hand and led her out to the floor. She was not as athletic as Anna, but she was good. Her sense of rhythm was good and she hooked him into her rhythm. He was happy, would have grinned if he could. What he did do was surrender to her rhythm and they danced well together.

It happened. In time, people stopped staring at him and realized he and his wife really liked to dance. Anna had won immediate acceptance, but Chris still had one more hurdle to jump. A classically beautiful young woman, no more than 17 or 18, named Grace Uris, was giving Chris the eye. He met her eye, gave his head a quick shake signaling no, and turned back towards Anna. He didn't catch the nod of approval the young girl cast at Evergreen, but Anna did.

Later, Grace approached Anna. "Would it be all right with you if I danced with your husband?"

"You can ask him."

She did.

Chris leaned back, looked Grace in the eye, and said, "Why me?"

"Cause I never danced with a scary scar-faced ugly old white man before."

He nodded and said, "Sounds about right and I'm not as old as I look." He offered her his arm, and she took it.

After the dance, Grace said, "I can't read your face. You never smile."

He put one finger on his cheek and said, "Can't. Scar tissue. There's a disconnect between my emotions and my face. I can only smile on the inside."

• • •

Dave Everguard approached. "Would you and your wife join me in the office?" Seated, he said, "You comfortable with being the only white allowed in this club and not ever mentioning the existence of this club?"

"I'm grateful for the chance to get away from my colleagues, away from the press, away from the job. Like it says in the commercial, "Oh what a relief it is."

CHAPTER SEVENTEEN—Pregnant

Seattle rains. Two to three months a year the weather is beautiful, but the rest of the time it rains—not heavy but constant. Landlord and retired-cop Frank Betger, outside his basement door, had poured a cement patio floor and built a roof to keep the rain off his Atlas exercise machine and the punching bag. The two of them, Frank and Chris, worked out together. Greenlake and it's bicycle path was only nine blocks away, and Chris again took up jogging, his stamina had returned after a long absence and once again very few would even try to keep pace with him.

"Chris" Betger said, "You like being a supervisor?"

"I liked the adrenaline rush of being the one doing things, got addicted to that overseas, and I miss that being alive feeling sometimes, but now I'm caught up in seeing that things get done. It's quieter, not as big of a rush, but it's enough."

• • •

Chris received a call from the FBI office in Portland. Supervisor Floyd Costa said, "We have a stoolie down here who said that the word on the street is that Marty Hogan and Rich Rinzler have pulled off a big score. We were watching when Rinzler made a purchase at Walmart, paid for it with a hundred-dollar bill, left the store with the purchase and the receipt, then he returned the purchase and got his refund. He pulled the same money laundering stunt at Cosco. Serial numbers on both bills indicate they were from the Portland armored truck robbery. That, plus Hogan's fingerprint, was enough. We arrested them. The drive from Portland to Seattle is 175 miles, they'll learn about the Portland evidence we have and then we'll transfer them to your office in Seattle."

. . .

Hogan and Rinzler had not been told where they were being transported, but it was clear that they were heading up US Highway Five. Having had time to think they concluded, as they were supposed to conclude, that they were being indicted for the Seattle payroll job. They asked each other, "How did they find out?"

. . .

Chris knew Agent Harvey Isler well; he called Isler to his office. "Harvey," he said, you've worked with Agent Terry Neal and I don't know him. What can you tell me about him?"

Harvey hesitated. One does not speak ill of a fellow Agent, but he looked at the Agent in Charge and said, "He knows a lot about the banking system, has really studied it, understands it better than most of us, but what I don't like about him is that he's always trying to prove that he's smarter than you, he tries to set you up with sucker bets that will take money out of your pocket. It's not so much that he's after your money but it's his own smug sense of superiority that rankles."

"Uh huh. Well, you and I are going to give him another chance to prove how smart he is. He knows all about Marty Hogan and Rich Renzler, which is interesting since professionally, he's never been within a country mile of either one of them. What we have connecting Agent Neal to Hogan and Renzler is thin so we need to establish the evidence of their connection.

"I will inform Agent Neal that I am putting him in charge of interrogating those two, that they had bragged to a Police Informant about having committed two Armored Truck robberies, and that it is his job to get their confessions. It's a good thing my face doesn't register emotion because my delight in seeing his consternation would have tipped him off. Neal doesn't need to know that you're the Agent in Charge."

"So," Isler said, "Agent Neal is the pigeon you're after?"

"He is."

"One of our own. Jesus how I hate this!"

• • •

Harvey reported to Chris. "I was twenty feet back when Terry approached the cell holding Hogan and Renzler. I couldn't see it but I think he put one finger across his lips signaling sssh, and announced, "I'm FBI Agent Terry Neal.""

"That," Agent Isler said, "was when I beat my retreat."

Chris wagged his head, and said, "I would have loved to see the expression on their faces; I suspect they would have registered confusion. Definitely, a reduced sentence is in order if they nail Agent Neal for us."

Nodding, Agent Harvey Isler said, "They didn't let on how angry, how humiliated they were about being conned by Neal. I gave them the tape recorder, told them to badger Neal about how he was going to get them off while I impressed on them that he couldn't get them off, since he is as guilty as them, even guiltier, but what they can get is consideration for assistance in nailing a crooked FBI Agent. I told them it's their chance to get a much-reduced sentence."

Neal assured Hogan and Renzler that he could get every scrap of evidence thrown out of Court, they taped every word he spoke, and that was all the evidence they needed.

• • •

Agent Neal was called to the Office of Chris Cordel while Agent Harvey Isler and two other Agents were also in waiting.

Chris said, "Neal, you are under arrest!"

Agent Neal stared, "Wha-a-t?" He blustered, "What for? You scar-faced piece of shit, you can't arrest me!"

Agent Harvey Isler, usually a laid-back non-demonstrative man, slugged Neal in the pit of his stomach, hard enough to double him over, and said, "You're not worth the sweat off this man's balls, so show some respect. Hogan and Renzler taped you, and convicted bank robbers Walter and Edna Pearlman will be brought in to testify against you. You'll be eligible for Parole in about 200 years."

Each of the arresting officers was in a chilling cold rage, felt humiliated by Agent Terry Neal's betrayal of their office, they hated him for it… and were unnecessarily rough as they relieved him of his weapon, hand-cuffed and ankle-cuffed him. Animosity as well as contempt rang out as Chris said, "Get him out of my sight."

• • •

That night Chris said, "Anna, Hogan and Renzler taped Neal from their jail cell, and convicted bank robbers Walter and Edna Pearlman will be brought in to testify against him. He'll be eligible for Parole in about a 100 years. Isler is usually a very contained Agent. Why did he lose it and slug Neal?"

"Chris, you silly ass, Neal was never one of them. You're one of their own and you are much admired, much loved. Him calling you a scar-faced piece of shit, that was one more mistake he made."

Neal had not been taken by elevator up to the sixth floor and into lockup. Instead, he was paraded out of the building and out onto Fourth Avenue and paraded on the sidewalk down James Street and around the building to the entrance on the Third Avenue side of the building; and that was when he broke down and began sobbing.

Isler told Chris, "Neal couldn't handle it, wet his pants, and he was sobbing by the time we entered the building and took the elevator up to lockup."

• • •

Chris embraced Anna and said, "I have some feeling back in my lips. Feeling your lips on mine, as much as I can, is wonderful. What I miss the most though, even before I ever touched you, is that I could then smell the sweet scent of you. God how I miss that."

When they broke from their embrace Anna said, "So now you can take me to dinner and then take me dancing."

• • •

Chris and Anna were driving to Spokane. Anna had lived in Seattle all her life but had never been as far East as the few miles to

Snoqualmie Falls. Stopping to view the Falls, and eating at the restaurant above the Falls, she was amazed to find this marvel so close to where she had spent her entire life. Continuing up and over the Snoqualmie Pass entranced her. Back down on the flat again, Anna said, "I saw on the map. We'll be passing through Cle Elum where your old girlfriend lives, are we going to stop to see her?"

"I'm thinking on it. I like Lucy and her parents, like them a lot. I haven't decided… probably not."

Chris didn't slow down as they passed the two exits off Interstate 90 into Cle Elum. Neither of them spoke until they were well passed Ellensburg. Anna said, "You didn't stop."

"It would very likely have been the last time I'd ever see them and I'd just as soon leave them remembering me the way I was rather than the way I am now. I'm still self-conscious about my appearance but that is fading.

Anna's eyes were big as they passed a field of huge electricity-generating wind turbines. "We're now starting down into the Columbia Gorge." We could coast," Chris said, "for the next nine miles if we wanted to, all the way to the bridge crossing the Columbia River."

Halfway up the gorge on the other side of the bridge they pulled into the parking lot, stepped out of the car and took the path to the viewpoint looking over the Columbia River gorge."

Anna's eyes were everywhere on this bare land. Seeing the sign warning about rattlesnakes, she stayed on the pavement, but she loved the view.

Back on Highway 90, up and out of the Columbia Gorge and onto the flatlands of Eastern Washington, Anna said, "There's so much to see that I've never seen. It blows my mind."

Passing by the last exit out of Ritzville, Chris got a look at a young man with his thumb out. Chris slowed and fifty yards east of the young man he pulled off to the side of the highway. He said, "Anna, climb over the back seat and get down. Now!" When she had done so he honked his horn.

On hearing Chris honk his horn the young man turned. On seeing Chris had stopped, the young man started jogging towards the car but seeing the car now gliding off-road back towards him, he jumped across the small ditch and waited. When the car stopped opposite him he jumped back across the ditch, lowered his head and looked in as the window rolled down. "Holy Shit!," he said, "What happened to you?"

"Get in. How far you going?"

"Billings. I got a job waiting for me there… sorry about my spouting off like that."

Not unkindly, Chris said, "Yeah. You probably need to think first before you open your yap."

"I agree. My name is Charlie Frey. Why'd you stop for me?"

"I'm FBI. You looked like someone we're looking for but you're not him. Anna, you can get up now."

When Anna's head popped up directly behind him, Charley Frey let out a startled, "Wooh!" Then he laughed. "My nerves are shot."

"When we get to Sprague," Chris said, "you and my wife will swap seats."

They drove to Spokane, passed through, and let Charlie out at a spot where he could continue hitchhiking East. Anna dropped a twenty on him, and then Anna and Chris headed back into downtown Spokane and to the FBI Field Office.

The Officer-in-Charge of the Spokane Office, Larry Friedman, was 62 years old, had a wife, two children, and four grandchildren. A big man, crew cut and overweight, he and his wife Lulu were looking forward to his upcoming retirement. They took Chris and Anna out to dinner. "Chris," Friedman said, "Shakespeare spoke of Romeo and Juliet as 'star-crossed-lovers who lost their lives.' You two have been star-crossed-lovers, alright, but unlike in the play, the children are the survivors, while it was the parents who died. Each of you have taken one hell of a beating but you survived. Why? I believe that you have been spared for some reason, and I suspect that the last dance will be yours."

Then the four of them went dancing. The scar-faced white man along with the black girl with the flashing eyes, were not only a different looking couple, but they could dance. Once that was established, Chris danced with Lulu and Anna danced with Larry.

That night Lulu and Larry put them up in the spare bedroom. Lying in bed, Chris said, "Anna, I'm not a spiritual person, you are, I'm not, and I don't know how to respond to all this acceptance."

"Chris, for God's sake, look at what you've done. You manipulated me, a half-crazed and uneducated angry street kid into going to college, and now, despite my having a juvenile record, I hold a Masters Degree in Social work, am a Probation Officer, carry a badge and a gun, and despite you being one of the toughest men on the planet, I even boss you around from time to time. You were the father I never had when I needed a father, and the husband I needed when I needed a husband.

"Ritch, I'm pregnant and looking forward to being the mother of your child. I know absolutely nothing about parenting a child, so that child and I will sorely need you."

"And I do? Anna, we've both got a lot to learn."

• • •

Morning came and during breakfast Lulu said, "Anna, will your baby look like you or like Chris?" They looked at her. "Whoops, what I said."

"Relax," Chris said, "We know what you meant and you are forgiven. Anna's mother was white, I'm white, our baby may or may not be lighter than Anna but will definitely not look like me."

CHAPTER EIGHTEEN—Monroe Reformatory

Chris had called the recommended Agency for a nanny. He cautioned, "I'm FBI so don't send me anyone who doesn't have the proper papers."

The Agency sent Nanny Rosita Garcia who was 44 years old, widowed, had already raised her two children who were now living in Puerto Rico, had a brilliant smile and was full-figured. Anna and Rosita met and right from the beginning the two of them hit it off. On the 20th of October, Anna gave birth to a beautiful baby girl she named Chenai. While Chris had secretly hoped for a boy, when he saw Chenai he capitulated completely and kept repeating, "She's perfect, just perfect." Definitely, Chenai looked like her mother and had her mother's complexion.

When mother with daughter returned home, Rosita had everything in order.

Then Chris received a call from Lucy Ballard. "So Chris, you're now a proud papa."

"That I am. That why you called?"

"Chris, I need your help. My boyfriend, Herm Borchardt, is much troubled about the relationship I had with you. When I said that the two of you are alike in some ways he sort of came unglued, looked shocked, said I didn't even see him. Would you meet with him?"

"That what you want?"

"That's what I want."

"Not at the office. At my home."

• • •

Herm Borchardt drove up, parked in front of the house on East 60th and three blocks west of Aurora Avenue. Herm was a slender and gentle appearing man. Anna noted that his first look at Chris's face elicited curiosity, possibly sympathy, but not revulsion. Right off, Anna and Ritch liked him. Seated in the dining room with coffees in front of them, Herm said, "I don't even know why I'm here. Lucy is deluding herself. She's said we're alike and we're not the least bit alike. You were whipping on Lucy's ass. I've never whipped on a girl's ass, I never will, you've destroyed people waving samurai swords and firing automatic weapons while I've been in one fist fight in my life and got my ass kicked. How can she possibly think we're alike?"

On cue, Chenai stirred in her crib and gave a small cry. Chris arose, lifted her from the crib, checked her diaper, put her on his shoulder and burped her. She went back to sleep. Chris said, "We're more alike than you realize."

"Oh my God," he said. "You protect. So obvious, and I missed it."

Anna said, "Whut you gonna do Herm?"

Chris chuckled, "First time in years I've heard my wife drop back into street talk."

Herm thought on it and nodding, he said, "What I'm going to do is drive back to Cle Elum, drop down on my knees, and ask that girl to marry me."

• • •

"Chris," Anna said, "the Diversion con's I get from the Monroe Reformatory are less hard-core than the cons I get from Walla Walla Prison, and yet the cons from Monroe are the ones running off and getting loaded. I suspect that something is fundamentally wrong and I don't know the what of it."

"You recognized something's wrong. That's a good beginning… that's where we start."

Chris dialed up his secretary. "Jill, I have to run up to Monroe. Anything come up you give me a call."

Anna stared. "You're coming with me?"

"I'll follow you up."

•••

Chris sat silent in the Monroe Reformatory Conference Room while Anna and Monroe staff discussed Inmates being considered for placement. Officer Bingham appeared relaxed and self-confident as he reported, "I work with the Trustees maintaining the grounds outside the fence. You get to know what works with each of them. Trustee Bell is my best worker, does twice the work of the others, but when he gets on my nerves, which he does sometimes, I send him off to the other side of the field to work alone and that solves the problem."

He looked at Anna and said, "You might want to think about that if you take him into your Program."

With that remark, Anna noted that Chris had looked at his watch. On exiting the gate, Anna said, "I saw you glance at your watch. I see you do that sometimes to indicate you're not really interested in what's being said."

Chris nodded. "You saw it. I have a book on the life of Joe Louis. Prior to the first Schmeling/Louis fight, Schmeling said in his German accent, 'I see somesing.' I didn't see somesing, but I did hear something. What Schmeling had seen was that Joe Louis sometimes dropped his left hand, leaving an opening for a straight right hand. Plus in their first fight, Joe had regarded Schmeling lightly and Schmeling staggered Louis in the first round, continued pummeling Joe with right hands, and gave Joe a terrible beating. Joe Louis and his people corrected those faults and in the first round of their rematch Louis damn near killed Schmeling and put him in the hospital for the night."

"You heard or saw something?"

"Maybe... I think so. I'll see you at the house."

That evening Chris called Warden Manchowitz at his home. After identifying himself he said, "Warden, I think I spotted a way drugs are coming into the Prison."

●●●

Chris dispatched a crack FBI Surveillance Team to Monroe… It took a few days but they filmed it all. Trustee Bell was filmed bugging Officer Bingham, which prompted Bingham to order Bell to the other end of the field and all alone. Long distant camera's had picked up where the small piece of red rag was tied to the fence marking the location of the drugs. Trustee Bell was apprehended with the drugs in his possession. Officer Bingham was also taken into custody as a suspected accomplice, his having been the one to send Bell off alone to where the drugs were. He was not considered a suspect, just a dummy, but they were pissed at him for embarrassing them and gave him the full treatment as if he truly were a suspect.

Three days of accusing him of taking payoffs, of being guilty of negligent homicide in providing the drugs that led to killing overdoses, had left Bingham a shaken and quaking wreck who confessed, "I'm not a co-conspirator, I was a patsy!"

Warden Mankowitze said, "I have no sympathy for Bingham's distress, none at all. Two things, first, people have died because of Bingham's smug stupidity, and second, Corrections Officers seeing the harsh interrogation Bingham's going through for his carelessness, for his stupidity, and the blistering evaluation I'm providing to justifying his firing, it serves as a lesson to others that this could damn-well happen to them, so they need to think, to stay alert."

Know-it-all smugness was quickly recognized as synonymous with stupidity, much like the criminal pride of the offender.

Other Officers had no sympathy for ex-officer Bingham. They were embarrassed by their former acceptance of him as an Officer who knew what he was doing. It became an axiom that smugness could only be maintained at the cost of not recognizing when you were being conned.

CHAPTER NINETEEN—Vacation

"Anna," Chris said, "I'm worn out, have nothing left to give. I think, if it weren't for you and Chenai, I'd probably lay down, pull a blanket up over my head and let it all go by."

"Chris, most would call this depression, but I think you're right. You're worn out. All that stress. Twice in Afghanistan you escaped death by the narrowest of margins, plus you lost most of your hearing over there. You have trouble sleeping, have nightmares. Unarmed, you took on a samurai-wielding madman and after surviving that you had your face blown all to hell. No one but you could have survived that injury—then you had to survive the surgical repair jobs."

"That's not all of it," Chris said.

"What," Anna said, "You losing some of the hearing in your other ear? I knew that was going on even before you did. Eventually, you will need a hearing aid for both ears plus you need reading glasses. What you also need is a vacation. You have a ton of money but you're too damn cheap to spend any of it so I booked us a luxury cruise. I've already cleared it with Director Holbrook and my boss, it's all been paid for, so Rosita, Chenai, you and I are going to take the luxury cruise up to the Arctic Circle; it's the vacation we both need and Rosita will also have a chance to go play when we relieve her."

• • •

The Cruise Ship Sea Breeze was a world unto its own, had a photo–op mentality and ship photographers were everywhere. Anna contacted the Captain and said, "Under no circumstances will your crew photograph my husband's face."

Their cabin, C12, was on the third deck, had a fake marble-surround Jacuzzi tub and with a shower in the tub. The Sea Breeze had four decks and for sure, this cruise ship was no small potatoes.

Always the policeman, Chris pondered the crew. It seemed to him that there was a strong caste system, at least on this cruise ship, and the crewmen who did the grunt work were of Far Eastern Extraction, either Chinese or Korean, while room attendants and kitchen help, plus the servers in the Buffet area, appeared to be from the Philippines. The waiters appeared to be Italian or Portuguese, while the headwaiters and maître D's were Italian. The crisp white uniforms who worked behind the purser's desk, those who manned the cash registers and concessions, gift shops and bars, appeared to be British or American. The Captain and other Ship's Officers were Italian.

Lunchtime, they were crossing the Queen Charlotte Sound toward the Gulf of Alaska.

Having entered the Cruise ship's plush, chandelier-draped dining room for lunch, Anna and Chris were seated with the Hawkins family, who were obviously uncomfortable at being seated with a scar- faced white man and his African/American wife. Anna was furious and that made them even more uncomfortable. She frightened them when she said, "My husband is a high-ranking FBI Agent. If he starts looking at the Hawkins family, do you think he might find something?"

Mister Hawkins had an attack of coughing. Chris then made a decision, after he returned to his office, he would take a look at Mister Hawkins.

Dinner-time, maitré d Rinaldi had already moved to inform Anna and Chris that their seating arrangement had been modified and that they would be seated with the Randolph family at table 4D. They were informed that the other family seated there were from Seattle and were looking forward to meeting them. When they arrived at table 4D, the man arose, reached out his hand and said, "John Randolph." When Chris took his hand John said, "Everyone in Seattle knows who the two of you are and we are delighted to meet you. This is my wife Marion, our daughter Vanessa, and our son Jesse. They all shook hands. Vanessa, they guessed, was probably 17 or 18 while brother Jesse appeared to be a year or two younger.

The food and company were excellent. After dinner, Jesse and Vanessa joined up with a group their own age while Marion looked at Anna and said, "I saw, you recognized it." Anna nodded. Neither of the men made a comment.

When they were alone, Chris said, "What did you pick up on?"

"I'm older than Vanessa but she's attracted to me, not you, her brother saw it, and him grinning, he's comfortable with it, I think the two siblings confide in each other, and both, I think, may have sometimes been attracted to the same girl. The boy and his sister are friends."

It was a beautiful night. John said, "There's a musical in the theater, there's a pianist/comedian in the Twilight Lounge, and there's a Jazz Combo in the Columbia Lounge."

The Columbia Lounge it was, and they danced. On the break, John said, "Would you allow me to dance with your beautiful lady?" If Chris had been capable of smiling he would have. Instead, he placed Anna's hand on John's arm. They danced well together, but Anna, being younger and the firecracker she is, after a time a grinning John cried mercy and said, "You've worn me down." At the close of the dance, John's grinning 16 year-old son Jesse, marched up and said, "Dad, would you allow me to cut in on you?" John looked to Anna who nodded assent, and danced off with young Jesse.

Chris took note of daughter Vanessa. She was tall, slender, had beautiful arms, beautiful legs, a pale complexion topped with a glorious mop of wavy brown hair. While Anna might be classified as a firecracker, Vanessa, on the surface, was languid. Then Vanessa cut in on her brother. "Anna," will you dance with me?"

They danced off together, raising a few eyebrows that quickly evaporated into shrugs.

John's wife Marion said. "Our spouses and our children seem to have deserted us." Chris nodded, cocked his head, and offered his arm. She took it and to her relief, Chris offered her a more sedate mode of dance. After the number was over, Marion said, "Our daughter is not a threat to you."

"I know."

• • •

The following evening, following the long visit with daughter Chenai, the Cordels again met with the Randolphs and went dancing. They had danced for the full set and Anna and Chris were sitting in front of their non-alcoholic drinks while the Musicians were taking their break.

That was when Phillis and Arthur Sandow made their entrance. Chris noticed them and turned his head away. "Anna," he said, "my distant eyesight is still pretty good and makeup does not conceal the bruises. That guy kicked the crap out of her since we saw them this morning. We came here for a vacation and once again we run into some asshole."

"You're facing away at 90 degrees while I'm seated facing in his direction. He's noted your scarred face and has already provided me with a nod of sympathy for my plight, my having a damaged husband. The son of a bitch is looking at me as a possible conquest."

Vanessa, hearing this, leaned forward, then leaned back and said, "None of you saw it, please don't look in his direction, but earlier today he was hitting on me."

"Anna," Chris said, "You up for teaching him a lesson?"

"If it will help lift you out of this blue funk you've been in for the last two months, hell yes. Let's do it." The Randolph's heard this, but didn't ask.

The next day, Arthur Sandow approached Anna. With a wistful smile he said, "What ever happened to romance? I have a wife who drinks too much and you have a scarred husband who doesn't even see you. How did this happen to us?"

Anna thought, *this line is so pathetic I want to puke. I wonder if it ever worked?* What she said was, "My husband will be playing in the Bridge Tournament at 2 PM tomorrow. Show up at Cabin C12 at that time and I will introduce you to delights you have never known."

Arthur showed up at the stroke of 2 PM, gave one knock on the door, Anna, nude, opened the door, took one look up and down the hall, grabbed him by the shirt and dragged him inside while saying, "Get out of your clothes Sweetheart. You can't imagine how much I want you."

When Arthur stepped out of his sandals, ripped off his shirt and stepped out of his shorts, Anna said, "Chris," and Chris came out of the bathroom. Arthur threw a feeble but pointless punch as Chris spun him around, trapped Arthur's arm up behind his back, walked him out into the hallway, released Arthur and returned to his suite while Anna locked the door behind him. They heard a shriek from down the walkway. Someone called the front desk, and reported, "There's a nude man running around on C Deck."

Chris gathered up Arthur's clothes, walked out to the deck, and threw them overboard.

• • •

The next day Captain Cardona paid Anna and Chris a visit. He was a handsome man, taller than Chris, and his voice was a rich baritone. He said, "Mister Cordel, I and my Crew are aware of the esteem with which you are held within your own country. We are not stupid. Despite Mister Arthur Sandow's self-serving account of what happened, we have a pretty good idea of what really happened. We do not like scandal and as a professional courtesy, we will not ask you questions which would put you in a position where you would be obliged to lie to us."

"Uh huh." Chris said. "Phillis Sandow, his wife—how's she holding up?"

"We put her in contact with her parents yesterday. She was put up in a vacant unit for the night, and her parents have made arrangements to have her flown out when we dock. Mister Sandow is having a difficult time since his identification, his credit cards and his money are missing."

That night the unease and the world weariness that had been so close to overwhelming Chris—it dissolved. He drifted into a sense of peace and felt some of the serenity akin to what Anna derived from her AA Meetings. Only in his sleep did Chris appear troubled.

The two of them spent most of the day with their daughter Chenai and that provided Rosita with her longest daytime opportunity for shipboard exploration and romance. From the look on her face when Rosita returned, it was evident she had not wasted that time.

Chris was experiencing a sense of serenity, something he hadn't felt in months. The why of it he couldn't say.

CHAPTER TWENTY—Anna's Confession

"John," Chris said, "My wife, when dancing to jazz, will offers little mercy. As you have learned, she will take the lead and even a marathon man would have difficulty keeping up with her."

"That what you love about her?"

"One of many things."

"Marion and I have noted the accepting way you relate to our daughter. Why is this?"

"Because she's a neat kid, very accepting of us even though we are a different kind of couple. We like her, like both your kids. We dock in Skagway in the morning. You and your family plan to take that narrow-gauge railway trip up White Pass?"

"We do."

"Anna and I have already signed up for it, and we will see what we will see."

In Skagway, the Sea Breeze had no sooner docked when the overcast sky began pouring down rain. Once aboard the train, a woman passenger broke out her travel brochure and pointing, said, "That's where the museum is, that's where they display what the gold rushers had to take with them on the way up the trail to Lake Bennett."

As the train headed up out of Skagway, the rain was so thick that there was not much else they could see. When the sun started burning through the clouds the lady with the brochure pointed and said, "That's the Chilkoot Trail. Before the railroad was built, that was the only way to get to Lake Bennett.

Sunshine then burst through the clouds and they caught sight of more traces of the Chilkoot Trail.

When they return to Skagway all were tired and hungry. The Cordel/Randolph party of six entered a sturdy no frills and less-than-posh restaurant and bar, took seats, and ordered six of the House Specials. Four Indians were on one side of the room and five whites were on the other. Each group was pumping themselves up for a physical confrontation. Chris arose from his chair, chin down but eyes up, he glided left and right between the two groups. John Randolph started to rise but Anna put her hand on his arm and said, "No don't. Sit, watch, and you'll see something."

Both groups faltered. One of the whites looked at Chris and said, "You don't frighten me."

Anna let out a guttural laugh and said, "Go ahead, get stupid! You won't be the first!"

The groups… confused, broke up and then drifted back to their seats. Chris's shoulders drooped, his hands fluttered, he sighed and returned to their table. The owner showed up.

"Folks," he said, "the steaks are on the house."

John said, "Chris, You're beautiful."

Chris laughed, "Nobody ever calls me that."

The steak dinners were excellent.

• • •

The Sea Breeze began the return trip to Seattle.

That afternoon the winds died down, the clouds rolled away, the seas returned to relative calm and the views were spectacular. Anna and Chris were close enough to the back of the ship that they could see the glow of the phosphorescence churned up in their wake.

Turning from staring at the wake, Anna leaned into Chris and announced, "Chris, you did it again. I'm pregnant."

• • •

On returning to Seattle, first things first, Chris learned that his secretary, Jill Johanson, had laid out all the paperwork that needed his signature. Harvey Isler had been Agent-in-Charge of case management during Chris's absence. "Harvey," Chris said, "you're as good an executive as me but you don't have my celebrity."

"You're stuck with that, while me, I don't want it and don't need it; not for the next five years anyway. When I get up close to my retirement I'll opt for advancement so as to up my retirement pay, but meanwhile, I'd like to stick to the shadows."

"Harvey, you are one damn fine Agent."

• • •

Director Holbrook called. "How soon will you be free to join me in DC?

"Wednesday."

"That's soon enough. See you then."

• • •

During lunch, Director Holbrook said, "The Democrats will nominate Ellis for President. He's a little too far to the left for my taste, but he is a smart and decent family man who would do us no harm. The Republicans have two potential nominees. Stegall is a good man, is stable, knows the system, and gets the job done. His rival for the nomination, Kern, is charismatic, has a ton of money, and I'm handcuffed, I can't release the fact that I know he's unstable. God help the Nation if he gets the nomination and wins."

Chris was confronted by reporter Terry Abbott, who followed as Chris hurried away. "Mister Cordel, who do you support in the Presidential Election?"

"You agree to blur my face in this newscast?"

"We do."

"Okay. You have no idea how little interest I have in politics, in who gets the Presidency. The majority of the citizens who know far more than I do will answer that question. I fight the nation's battles on the field of battle and in the streets. That's all I do. I know nothing, care nothing, about politics or politicians."

Abbott said, "O-k-a-y, so let's take it from there. How would you rate each of them as a combat soldier?"

Chris's pace slowed. "Ellis, I suspect, would be a good warrior.

John Stegall, how should I say this… I saw men like him in Afghanistan, men not necessarily born warriors, but men you could count on to hold things down, to manage, to be steady, to act decisively and hold things together, get things done, make the right decisions."

Newscaster Abbott continued, "As a soldier, how would you rate Candidate Kern?"

Chris's face does not register emotion, but his stiffened body spoke volumes. His voice dropped, and he said, "I wouldn't," and walked away.

• • •

Holbrook reviewed that tape for the umpteenth time. Each time he heard Chris say, "I wouldn't," Holbrook chuckled.

"Chris, how did you know to do that?"

"You clued me in on Kern and I have battlefield experience. You didn't say it directly but I knew what you wanted plus the fact that I have had experience with officers like Kern. I spoke from experience."

"Experience?"

"Experience. I once had a Captain, when the shooting started, turned his helmet around so his two bars wouldn't be showing, then hid in a ditch."

• • •

Ballard, the Seattle neighborhood where the Randolph family lived, was not an upscale neighborhood, but the homes on the west side of 34th Street were perched on the steep bank overlooking Elliot Bay, provided a view of the Olympics… and those homes were definitely upscale.

The Randolph family, all four of them, were living on the middle-class East Side of NW 34th Street. John called Chris and said, "You and Anna are both holding down important jobs and you being ready to move out of the Wallingford District, you really need to take a look at this property on the West Side of 34th Street. It'll go on the market in a few days. It's across the street and the third house to the north of us."

Anna and Chris walked to the back of the property, looked down the steep bank to the railway tracks running alongside the shoreline road and then stared across the road to the Marina where small pleasure craft were docked. Looking across Puget Sound, the sun was just beginning to set behind the Olympic Range. Anna wrapped her arms around Chris and kissed him on the cheek. They entered the house, didn't speak while the Agent prattled on about it's features and it's furnishings. They looked at each other, Anna grinned, nodded, and Chris wrote out a check for the full price.

• • •

Chris's cellphone rang. He listened, then without speaking, with cellphone to ear, he retreated to a back bedroom. Returning, he said, "I have work to do. They're sending a car for me and I don't know when I'll be back."

Out front, they heard the honk of a car horn. As Chris was headed for the door, he heard Vanessa, who had been visiting, ask, "Does this happen often?"

"It happens anywhere from four to ten times a year.."

• • •

Chris returned at 1:05 AM. Anna roused herself from the couch and both retreating to the kitchen, Anna poured them coffee while Chris asked, "How'd it go after I left?"

"About like you'd expect. I informed Vanessa that enough feeling has returned to your lips that you can now feel a kiss, that you're still a lousy kisser but that I like kissing you anyway."

"You said that?"

"I did. She sort of broke down. Confessed that she was a lesbian, had crushes on women, including me, hungered for a relationship but had never had more than her one disastrous attempt to connect in a hetero relationship. Her dilemma is whether or not to come out of the closet, let it be known that she's a lesbian, said this is a conservative neighborhood, her parents live here, and she is conflicted about what to do."

"What did you tell her?"

"That we would be supportive of her and her family whatever she decides. How can I say this? I told Vanessa that one of the new words I learned when I left the streets was acceptability. I love that word. I was thirteen when Mom died. Mabel took me in and pimped me out. Mable was tough, mean, had a knife and would cut you in a heartbeat. Back then, most of what Mabel had me doing I accepted but some of it was beyond what was acceptable and that led me to flee Mabel and her protection.

"I told Vanessa that you and I see her as competent, steady, not a warrior and not a rebel.

"She thinks her coming out would embarrass her family. After Vanessa left, about fifteen minutes later, Mother Marion showed up. How I became the neighborhood relationship counselor I don't know, could it be because my pregnancy is showing? But Marion, hearing my report of Vanessa's concern for her family… hearing this, Marion dropped her eyes and said, 'it's a role reversal when the child feels she needs to protect the parents.'"

"Marion," I said, "Unless your family, all of you, find Vanessa having a relationship with another female acceptable, she's not going to come out of the closet. What I said to Vanessa is that she could play the field, or she can connect with someone who's hot but is also someone she would like to spend her life with, someone who would be acceptable to her family.

"I told her relationships on the gay scene evolve quickly and frequently too casually, so I told her to take her time; to think about it."

"Hah," Chris said, "You giving Vanessa, through her mother, permission to go slowly, in reality, you've given Vanessa permission to step it up, to do something."

"I think so… I hope so."

• • •

Chris and Anna were having lunch at the Pink Poodle when his cellphone rang. When he hung up, Anna said, "So you have a new case?" He nodded. "Is it local."

"It's not. I'll be going on the road."

"How come? You're the Agent in Charge. I'm pregnant so can't you send someone else?"

He shook his head. "I can't. He says he won't talk to anyone but me."

• • •

Chris usually enjoys the drive out of Seattle up and through the Snoqualmie Pass. On this occasion his mind was occupied with thoughts of Anna's pregnancy. Their second child was expected to arrive in about four weeks and Chris was expected to be there.

Chris thought, *So much is going on.* Exiting Interstate 90 at Ellensburg onto Hwy 82 South, his thoughts then returned to the upcoming case.

• • •

Entering Walla Walla Prison is a noisy and loud downer. As hard of hearing as he was, Chris still turned down his hearing aids. He was escorted to an interview room where Kurt Ueland was cuffed to the table. Chris sat, the Guard left, and Chris said, "So tell me why I'm here?"

"Because," Ueland said, "ten years ago you executed the wrong man. It was me killed Catherine Toole and her bastard son."

"Why you telling me this?"

"I'm never getting out of here, I have a son doing a nickel up in Monroe. I'd like him transferred here. Also, I killed Dan Brande. That case is still open and I can prove I killed the three of them. Plus, I can give you the sheriff who falsified the evidence that got David Toole executed. The hard evidence is the gun I used to kill three people."

"That was a long time ago. What makes you think that gun would still be preserved in a condition good enough to serve as evidence?"

"Because I have it sealed in a mason jar filled with oil."

"One more question. Why did you pull my name out of the hat?"

"It was you who got an FBI Agent a 100 year sentence for his part in a series of bank robberies."

"Uh huh. Tell you what Mister Ueland, if your information and your evidence checks out, whether he likes it or not, I'll get your son transferred from Monroe Reformatory to Walla Walla Prison."

• • •

Close up on the Spokane Indian reservation, the gun was where Ueland had said it would be and was still in mint condition. The bullet that killed Dan Brande had come from Ueland's gun.

Chris took a long look at the Toole case files. The records stated that the husband, David Toole, reported that he had arrived home at 9:14 PM, that the front door was locked, that he entered with his key and discovered the bodies of his wife and son.

• • •

"Sheriff Tate," Chris said, "Explain this to me. Officer Hodson, who was the original responder to David Toole's call, wrote a report stating that at 9:19 PM, he saw that there was evidence of a forced entry through the basement door. Yet your report at 12:50 AM contradicts Hodson's report. Your report states that there was no evidence of a forced entry."

Sheriff Tate said, "Officer Hodson was wrong. Toole had faked a forced entry and I corrected it."

"So you did. You never found the gun that killed the mother and child."

"We did not."

The lab tech then walked in and said, "The bullets that killed the woman and child are a match with the gun Ueland said he used to kill them."

Sheriff Tate's face paled. Chris looked at him. "You stacked the deck so an innocent man was executed. Resist arrest so I'll have an excuse for kicking your sorry ass."

Tate turned compliant and Chris returned to Walla Walla Prison. "Ueland," he said, "on our first meeting you admitted to killing Catherine Toole and her bastard son. Why bastard son?"

"Because noontime, I saw Catherine, I told her that she had no right to get married while I was up in Alaska, that we and our son belonged together, and that was when she told me I wasn't the father. I got all three of them, Catherine, David Toole, and their bastard son."

"She told you he wasn't your son to get rid of you. We have your DNA so we checked. The child you killed was your own son."

• • •

Leaving Walla Walla, glad to be out of there, Chris had cooled off enough that by the time he passed through Pasco that he was now ready to speak with his wife. He pulled off-road and parked before calling home. Rosita picked up, and said, "I'll get your wife."

Anna picked up. "Chris, you behind the wheel now?"

"I'm parked off-road. What's wrong?"

"Nothing's wrong. Our son Charley said he couldn't wait any longer and popped out this AM and almost two weeks before he was expected."

"You alright?"

"I'm fine and our son Charley is fine. Even though he was early he showed up weighing eight pounds two ounces. Chenai loves having a baby brother, says he's a beautiful baby."

• • •

Two weeks after Chris arrived home, John Randolph and wife Marion, along with son Jesse, paid a visit. After paying the proper homage to baby Charley, John said, "Chris, this girl Patrice that our daughter has taken up with, you've met her?"

"I have. Patrice said she wanted to meet with me and Anna first since that was easier than meeting the real parents. She looked me straight in the eye, didn't waver, and shook my hand. She has a great personality, is almost as tall as Vanessa and we like her."

"Chris, this involvement you and Anna have with our son and daughter, it's like you're a second set of parents. How did this happen?"

"We don't understand it either. We've always been in a crowd, but each of us have always felt disconnected, totally alone. How and why we connected emotionally with you and your family is something we don't understand, can't explain, but it happened and it feels good. We told Vanessa that we will fight to protect you and your family, but we will not put your daughter in a position where she would have to choose between us and her family. Family rules and we're only the reserves."

Jesse said, "You wouldn't fight for her?"

"Jesse, two dogs fighting over a bone, it's the bone that gets torn apart." The Randolph family were looking at each other. Heads nodded without speaking.

Anna said, "Chris and I will be in the back yard looking down on Elliott Bay."

• • •

The Randolphs joined them in the back yard. John shook his head, said, "I've always been a straight-laced conservative Catholic type guy. Why am I so comfortable, not shocked, with this? Is it by contagion? Is it because the two of you are comfortable with this?"

Son Jesse mumbled, "Because it's romantic Dad, not salacious."

They stared at him. Anna said, "Out of the mouths of babes."

John had to laugh and slapped his son on the shoulder.

• • •

There would be no trial for Ex-Sheriff Harold Tate. No defense of his actions could be mounted, he confessed, so they went directly to sentencing. Chris's presence was not needed, but he was glad to be there to hear Judge Cleaver, who said: "Mister Tate, you seem unable to resist maligning David Toole, the man you condemned to death as being a man of little worth, as a man of little consequence, and thus you attempt to mitigate the heinousness of your offense.

By falsifying evidence you not only condemned an innocent man to death, you also set the true killer free to continue on his killing spree. You thought you were playing God when you distorted the evidence, but in truth Sir, you were playing the Devil, I sentence you to Life in Prison and without Parole. This Court is adjourned."

The gavel came down.

• • •

John Stegall, one of the Candidates that Chris had championed, won the Presidency. On February the First, Chris met with the President, who asked, "Chris, what are your thoughts about serving in my Cabinet as an Advisor?"

"I suspect it's not a good idea. I'm too controversial, and that would put each of us at risk."

The President nodded. "So you're already advising me. I suspect you're probably right that I can't afford this. However, what I would like to do from time to time, is sneak you into the White House and see it gets leaked to the press that you met with the President. If the news media comes after you asking what we talked about what would you say?"

"I would say that the President asks me questions and I answer his questions and that is all I will say."

"Then they will ask you what were the questions the President asked, and you will say?"

"Ask the President."

"Wonderful. You understand the political clout that can be gained by not playing politics. Have a good flight back."

CHAPTER TWENTY ONE—Shot

In the University of Washington Hospital's cafeteria, Chris had lunch with Louis Johnson. "Louis," he said, "You know Anna and me. We're looking to you for a favor. On April 19, Vanessa Randolph will turn 19, and on that day, and with her families approval, it is her desire to enter into a union with Patrice Smith."

Louis raised his hand. "Why are you telling me this?"

"She would like, we would like, the Randolph family would like, a formal ceremony honoring the occasion of their handing their daughter over to Patrice. In the future laws will be passed that will legalize same-ex marriages but that day is not here yet and in the meantime Vanessa and Patrice would like a ceremony signifying their betrothal."

"Yes," Louis said, "I suppose they would. And you want me to perform this ceremony?"

"We do. We would like you to write it up, choreograph it, and perform the ceremony."

"Interesting. I'll look on the internet, check with Vanessa, her family, Patrice, you and Anna. I'll think on this, and then I'll get back to you."

• • •

The day, April 19, came. Louis was ready, the ceremony would take place in Chris and Anna's home, it being Roomy, and caterers would provide the meal. The Big Daddy Basque Quartet would provide the music. Rosita would be present and would help care for Chenai and Charley, and guests would include neighbors, Vanessa's parents and her brother.

Patrice's parents, being rabid Fundamentalist Christians, would boycott what they perceived as this bacchanalia.

At the closure of the ceremony Vanessa and Patrice exchanged vows, exchanged wedding bands and a long kiss. Vanessa, on breaking from the kiss gasped, "Finally! It's done."

Guests and musicians applauded.

The caterers had put out a fine meal. Anna and Chris, as a rule, allowed no alcohol in their home. On this occasion however, toasts were made in champagne while Anna, Chris, and minor children toasted with apple cider. The Big Daddy Basque Quartet played music they could dance to, and with the arrival of dusk, guests, musicians, and caterers departed.

• • •

"Chris," John said, "You don't seem to take offense when people refer to you as The Big Ugly, yet you do take offense when others take your photo. Why is that?"

"Referring to me as The Big Ugly may not be complementary, but it does humanize me. My feeling is that photo's dehumanize me."

Chris's next-door neighbor Steve Speiler said, "Chris, the way you look and your reputation for ferocity, plus your wife Anna being a true lady, but black and also ferocious, it being known that she came up from the mean streets–this gave hesitation to some. That, plus the fact we couldn't read the expression on your face, that alarmed us."

"Steve, the nerve damage, the scarring, much of what you see is resting on titanium implants. That has formed a disconnect between my emotions and my face."

"I know that now, but back then I didn't know. Plus, since then, in some way, you've learned, without facial movement, to give readable expression to your feelings through other body movements. Then you championed Vanessa and Patrice. That raised our curiosity, but by that time the alarm bells had been long muted."

"How come?"

"The evidence kept piling up, including Vanessa's parents living across the street, and them being our kind of people, their acceptance of you and Anna, plus we had watched Vanessa growing up, that reassured."

. . .

Chris's secretary, Jill Johansson, was six feet tall in her high heels, and a good looker. She said, "Chris, if Anna and my husband were to permit it, there would be a second beautiful women in your life."

"We don't get all the things we want in this life, which is probably a good thing, but if we did, then you'd be the second beautiful woman in my life."

"Chris, I don't believe you, but you saying it is so sweet."

. . .

Jill called and Anna picked up. "Anna, It's Jill from the office. Chris's been shot and they have him at the University Hospital. That's all I know so far."

Anna was hot-footing it across the U Dub campus when she saw Vanessa grabbed her, and they both headed at a trot for the U Dub Hospital. Vanessa gasped, "How bad is it?"

"I don't know."

"I'll call my parents. Mom and Dad will help Rosita with Chenai and Charley."

. . .

Louis Johnson came out of his office, intercepted Anna and Vanessa, and said, "He's in surgery, but he's been through worse than this. The shot tore up his lower rib cage on the right. That's all I know. Go to the cafeteria. Get a cup of coffee and wait. I'll see that someone comes and gets you so you'll be there when he comes out of surgery."

Anna and Vanessa were at his bedside when Chris groaned, opened his eyes, and Anna was holding his hand. He said, "Damn! Back in the U Dub Hospital."

"Seattle Detective Brundage said I'd be allowed to talk to you only after he'd received your report. I sort of lost it."

"Sort of!" Vanessa snorted. "I've never seen you so fierce."

"What did she do?"

"She threatened to remove his balls if he got in her way. I mediated, and they both calmed down."

"Good for you. Chris cast his eyes around the room and said, "Not the same room I had before. Anna... Brundage really does need my report, so let him in so I can give it and then get some rest.

• • •

Seattle Detective Brundage and FBI Agent Harvey Isler, with tape recorder, entered. "Tell us what happened."

"The last Friday of every month, at exactly 2PM, I enter Lab Tech for my blood draw. This time, before entering, I saw an older model ambulance parked in front, a new guy was on the desk and a new tech was there for the draw. She came at me with a syringe used to inject, not the one that makes a draw, so I grabbed her hand with my left and gave it a squeeze."

"Her right hand, Isler said, "is black and blue, swollen up like a boxing glove with fingers. What happened next?"

"Those two pulled guns and it was the OK Corral Shoot out all over again. I cuffed the girl to the door, called 911, and then things got fuzzy. What happened to the regular staff?"

"They're OK. They were tied up and stuffed into the storage room in back."

"What about the shooters?

Isler chuckled. "One shot each. You plugged each of them dead-center in the chest. The girl and both men have needle tracks. The girl is already going into withdrawal. What were they after?"

"I don't know. You guys get out of here. I'm tired."

• • •

The next day Doctor Tom Sharkey, the Surgeon who had put Chris's face back together, walked in and said, "Dammit Chris, we've got to stop meeting like this."

"You're right about that. How bad is it?"

"Not so bad. What were you up to this time?"

"My monthly blood draw. The other times I walked into it. This time it was personal. They were already there and waiting for me."

Seeing Doctor Sharkey exit Chris's room, Anna's face registered alarm. Vanessa said, "What's wrong?"

Anna charged up. "Sharkey, you on my husband's case?"

"Nah. I'm a plastic surgeon, not a trauma surgeon. I dropped by to say hello but also to get a look at how well my repair job was holding up. It's holding up well… is an example of my better work."

Vanessa got off her cellphone. "My parents," Vanessa said, "are relieving Rosita, taking time with Chenai and Charley, taking them everywhere and since they've freed up Rosita she has turned into a cleaning whirling dervish washing all the windows inside and out. My parents think of Rosita as a member of your family. I do too."

"So do we."

Anna kissed Chris, Vanessa kissed him, and the two women went home.

• • •

CNN Newscaster Goodman confronted Chris. "Mister Cordel, on the eighth of July, as the sun was setting, you were caught on film being sneaked into the White House to meet with President Stegall. The meeting with the President lasted for more than two hours. Are you being considered for a Governmental posting?"

"I don't think so. Not to my knowledge anyway."

"Then why were you in the Oval Office?"

"I'm an FBI Agent. I serve the country and I serve the President. He asks me questions and I answer them. In these films you're taking of me, have some respect and blur out my face before you show them."

"Sir, we are newscasters and it is our duty to report the news, but out of respect for you and your services to this country, respectfully Sir, your facial image will be blurred out."

CHAPTER TWENTY TWO—A Star is Born

Newscaster Morton Jenks said, "Mister Cordel, You've never agreed to be interviewed on TV before, so why now?"

They were filming from behind Chris and catching Chris from the back while catching Newscaster Jenks at full face. "The short answer to that is you're paying me a decent sum of money. The longer answer is that I have two children and I'm in process of setting up college funds for my children."

"You don't expect to be around when that time comes?"

"Life insurance companies won't touch me without premiums that stretch way beyond outrageous. I decided to make other plans."

"If," Morton said, "you changed your line of work, would your premiums drop?"

"I can't do that; I'm a man with limits. Even what I'm doing now, much of the time, is sheer drudgery. If it wasn't for the 10 percent that is an adrenaline rush then this job would be too much for me. Any other job and I'd have to be skydiving out of airplanes to jumpstart my adrenal system… and I don't like heights. Some see school years as the best years of their lives. I slept through much of it, couldn't stay awake, was even tested for narcolepsy. I don't have a sleep disorder, but I bore easily."

"Chris, you're a hero to many." Do you have heroes?

"I do."

"Who are they?"

"Homer Wardel comes to mind. He's dead now. He was my hero. He did things I could never do. Homer would be the first to admit he wasn't the smartest guy around, was diabetic and had a heart condition, yet he worked forty hours a week, for forty years, on the most boring job imaginable and for poor pay. Plus, he put in an additional eight hours a week as a night watchman. He put his two daughters and his son through trade schools before he died of heart failure. I get things done through an adrenaline rush but Homer ground it out every day despite being a sick man. The poet Walt Whitman would have referred to Homer as one of the Divine Average. He was that, and that makes him my hero."

Chris was never thought of as one of the divine average but with that broadcast he apparently caught on as a hero to the divine average.

• • •

Morton Jenks had Chris back on his show, and said, "We've received messages from viewers stating that they would like to hear more from you."

"If I'd known that I'd have asked for more money."

"Too late now. Since we now know what you'll work for you're too late. And aside from the fact you were in the military and then in law enforcement, you still have had what others would say is incredible bad luck."

"How so?"

"What I know is that you've had bombs set off close to you and lost three fourths of your hearing, you've been shot numerous times, and on one of those occasion your face was shot up so badly that it was a miracle you didn't die and that it took a countless series of surgeries to put your face back together. You even had a crazy man with a samurai sword come after you while you were unarmed and you came close to losing your left hand, even your life. These things were improbabilities and yet you had the bad luck to be there when they happened."

"Hah! You've raised a tricky question. My wife said, 'are you the unlucky one to run into them, or were they the unlucky ones to run into you? You're alive and they're dead.' Chris shook his head and said, "My wife does things like that, poses conundrums that make my head spin. How can I answer to that?"'

"I would think, with your reputation, people would be afraid to tangle with you."

"That reputation, is it lucky, or is it unlucky? Again, the question remains… does it make me safer or does it put me at risk?"

"How would it put you at risk?"

"That time when I was in jail, I had Inmates coming after me looking to build a reputation as the con who took down FBI Agent Chris Cordel. I have read about the Post Civil War old west. Our two most famous gunfighters during that period were Wild Bill Hickok and John Wesley Hardin, both of them, along with Jesse James, were backshot by men looking for the notoriety of having been the ones to kill them. Hickok had even predicted that he'd be backshot."

"Hickok and John Wesley Hardin," Newscaster Jenks said, "are they heroes of yours?"

"I'm lukewarm about Wild Bill but Hardin was everything I detested in a man."

CHAPTER TWENTY THREE—The Final Chapter

Anna and Chris, their daughter Chenai and son Charley, along with nanny Rosita, arrived at the Sands Resort on a beautiful beach in the Caribbean. Their luxuriant quarters looked out on the beach and they were able to watch sunrises and sunsets.

Rosita cast her eyes on where the beach boys were gathered and exited their company while Chris and family kicked off their shoes and went for a walk on the beach. Chris took four-year old Chenai's hand and walked her along the lapping edge of the waves. Chenai, a sometimes quiet child, was holding her father's hand and bouncing up and down splashing water and chortling in a state of sheer ecstasy, while Anna walked a few steps ahead of them, carrying son Charley while sometimes walking backwards.

It occurred to Anna that while her husband's face was incapable of registering a smile, his body language was screaming contentment. She said, "Chris, in that Broadcast you gave everyone a glimpse of the simplicity that is you. That part of you usually stays hidden."

"I gave them something to think about. I told them to think on it. I have been lucky enough to have known only moments when my life was at risk. Homer Wardel had so many health problems that he was risking death just walking across the street, yet he picked up his lunch bucket and showed up for work six days a week for forty years—until, one day he showed up for work—lunch bucket in hand, and dropped dead. I asked my audience to think on that."

"You were conning?"

"I'm no angel and so maybe I was conning, maybe it was an ego trip. But you think on this, somewhere along the line, sometime after we married, my comfortable persona as the noble and heroic survivor began to slip and I became discomforted with the uneasy suspicion that I may be one of life's winners rather than a heroic survivor. Where's the honor in being a winner? Was it the uneasy suspicion that I was losing something valuable? Was that what triggered the onslaught of that blue funk I was in? I don't know."

"Could you be a little more specific?"

"Having won this beautiful woman, having two beautiful children, true friends in the Randolphs, John, Marion, their two kids Jesse and Vanessa, not to mention her girlfriend Patrice, Rosita looking after us and our two kids, that put a serious hurt on my pride as the heroic and all alone survivor."

• • •

It had been a two- hour long drive. "John and Chenai were in the back seat, restless and oblivious to the seriousness of the upcoming event. Ritch pulled off the highway onto a dirt road, and a mile off the paved road he parked the car alongside an old, primitive, and unpainted building. Ritch turned to Anna, and said, "Ready?"

She said, "Ready," They exited the car, Anna opened the backseat door, Chenai and Charley poured out of the backseat and onto this primitive landscape.

Then they were ushered into the ramshackle and unpainted building where they were met by a tall gaunt man in patched coveralls who shook hands briefly with Anna and Ritch and then ushered the two children through the back door and into a fenced yard where the children were surrounded by excited and yapping puppies, each of whom insisted that the children pay attention to them. Chenai and Charley must have felt like they were in dog Heaven.

After about ten minutes, Anna said, "Would you like to take one of these puppies home with us?"

They would.

Choosing which puppy to take home was a serious matter and the children gave it their serious consideration. Eventually they agreed on a tan, long haired and pug-nosed small puppy who would never get very big, and who was particularly insistent that the children pay attention to him.

On the drive home there was much discussion of a name for the puppy. Ritch suggested, "Toby might be a good name for a dog."

Neither child cared for the name. Anna put her comforting hand on Chris's arm. Chenai giggled and said, "He keeps bouncing up and down." They settled on Bouncer as the pup's name.

Anna said, "We give to our children what we have, and hopefully, we can give them some of what we missed, and that I suppose is what's known as progress.

THE END